MURDER IN MEMORIAM

MURDER IN MEMORIAM

DIDIER DAENINCKX

Translated by Liz Heron

This is a work of fiction. Any similarity of
persons, places or events depicted herein to
actual persons, places or events is entirely
coincidental.

British Library Cataloguing in Publication Data
Daeninckx, Didier
Murder in memoriam. — (Mask noir)
I. Title   II. Series
843 [F]

ISBN 1-85242-206-8

First published as *Meurtres pour mémoire* by
Editions Gallimard, Paris. Copyright © 1984 by Editions Gallimard

This edition first published 1991 by
Serpent's Tail, 4 Blackstock Mews, London N4

Translation copyright © 1991 by Serpent's Tail

Typeset in 10/12pt Aster by AKM Associates (UK) Ltd, London

Printed in UK by JRDigital Print Services Ltd, KENT

*For Jocelyne
and Aurélie*

By forgetting the past,
we condemn ourselves to relive it

CHAPTER ONE

SAÏD MILACHE

The rain started falling around four o'clock. Saïd Milache went over to where they kept the turps, to wipe off the blue ink staining his hands. The order boy, a ginger-haired youth who already had his call-up papers in his pocket, replaced him alongside the Heidelberg.

Raymond, the machine-minder, had merely slowed down the press and he was now taking it back to its original speed. The posters piled up on the palette at a regular rate, to the dry clicking rhythm of the grippers releasing them. Now and then Raymond would pick up a sheet, fold it, check it for alignment, and then run his thumb over the print to make sure of the quality of the inking.

Saïd Milache watched him for a moment, then made up his mind to ask him for one of the poster proofs. He got changed quickly and left the workshop. The gate-keeper was walking up and down in front of the railings. Saïd handed him the leave pass he'd got that morning on the pretext of illness in the family. Three in less than ten days! It was time to call a halt.

The gatekeeper took the slip of paper and put it in his pocket.

— Well, Saïd, I'd say you're making them up! If this goes on, you won't even need to come in here any more, you'll be sending your authorisations in the post.

He just smiled. He got on quite well with his work-mates so long as he forced himself to make light of their endless comments.

Lounès would be waiting for him further on, at the corner of Passage Albinel. He had to cross the St Denis Canal and go past the wooden huts and corrugated iron shanties that had invaded the embankment. The bridge made a hump, and in fine weather you could see the whole of Sacré Coeur behind the massive red-brick chimney-stack of Saint-Gobain. He slowed down and had some fun dodging his head this way and that so as to position the Basilica on top of the mounds of sulphur cloud crowning the factory site. To get the right effect, sometimes he ducked down, paying no heed to the startled reactions of passers-by. Below on the quayside, a crane was hauling up blocks of metal from the hold of a barge, and a fork-lift truck took them off to the sheds at Prosilor.

He crossed avenue Adrien Agnès to cut into the dense street-grid of the shanty-town. The first houses still had a few French people living in them. Two old women carrying broad oilcloth shopping bags were loudly debating the relative merits of Dulcine oil and Planta margarine. The café-grocery Breton was empty except for a young boy playing pinball.

Rosa's, Marius's, Café de la Justice, The Snack, the Gasworks Bar. There now came a succession of cafés, restaurants and hotels, each shabbier than the one before. Over the years their proprietors had sold up to Algerians, who had kept the original trading signs.

The exception was the Djurdjura, the last Arab establishment before the Spanish quarter. Saïd pushed the glass door open and went into the vast room. The usual odour, a mixture of damp and sawdust, rose from the disinfectant-washed floorboards. About ten men sat in a group around the coal-fired stove, watching two domino-players.

Saïd leant on the bar without anyone taking any notice of him.

— Has Lounès come?

The owner shook his head and served him a coffee.

Through the window Saïd could see an imposing building, the most prominent in the district apart from the factories. In actual fact, only a bell-tower and its three bells indicated that this wasn't some workshop extension. He had only once crossed the threshold of the Santa Teresa de Jesús mission, as a guest at a Catalan workmate's wedding.

The chime as the door opened was drowned out by the clacking of dominoes on the formica-topped table.

— Hello, Saïd. I'm late; the boss didn't want me taking time off . . .

Saïd turned and placed a hand on Lounès's shoulder.

— The main thing is you're here. Let's go into the office, we've got an hour at most.

Now they were in a tiny room cluttered with crates and bottles. On a table, piles of papers and invoices surrounded a black telephone.

Saïd unhooked a picture that was a promotional free gift from Picardy Wines. He slid the frame off, and, with the utmost care, pulled out a sheet of paper concealed between the picture and the backing card. Lounès had taken a seat at the desk.

— Did you see, Reims won't make it. I'm sure they're going to blow the championship. Three-one against Sedan! Another game like that and Lens will be in front.

— We have more important things to do than talk about football. Get on the phone to the fifteen group leaders. Just tell them 'REX'. They'll know what it

means. Meanwhile I'll go and see the sector heads. Meet
me outside Pigmy Radio with the car in three-quarters
of an hour. Don't forget to put the list back where it
belongs.

．

Saïd and Lounès parked the 4CV in La Villette, on
boulevard MacDonald, just past the ring road bus stop.
Then they headed towards the metro entrance. An icy
wind was scattering dead leaves. It took no time for the
drizzling rain to soak through their thin jackets. The
Gardes Mobiles barracks seemed quiet, although the
parking area was packed full, with the blue Berliét vans
of the *Compagnies Républicaines de Sécurité*, the CRS.

A train was leaving the station. The ticket collector
made them wait for a moment before he punched their
tickets. Lounès went up to the metro map and pointed
out Bonne-Nouvelle station.

— We can change at Gare de l'Est, then at Strasbourg-
Saint-Denis. Or else through to Chaussée d'Antin?

— Chaussée d'Antin. It seems longer but we'll only
have to change once. We'll get there quicker.

At each of its stops the metro filled up with Algerians.
By Stalingrad it was packed; the few Europeans
exchanged alarmed glances. Saïd smiled. He suddenly
remembered the poster he'd asked Raymond for before
he left the printshop. He took it out of his pocket,
carefully unfolding it before he showed it to Lounès.

— Take a look at what I've been turning out on my
machine for the last two days!

Above a photo of Giani Esposito and Betty Schneider
was a brief announcement of Jacques Rivette's first
film; the title was splashed right across the poster in
blue lettering: PARIS BELONGS TO US.

— Do you realise, Lounès, Paris belongs to us.

— For a single evening . . . If it was up to me, I'd let them keep the whole of Paris, Paris and everything else, a little village in the Hodna.

— I think I know what it's called.

— Say it then!

Saïd turned serious.

— Make no mistake, if we're here this evening, it's for the right to grow old in Djebel Refaa.

.

At 7.25 pm on Tuesday, 17 October, 1961, Saïd Milache and Lounès Tougourd climbed the steps of Bonne Nouvelle metro. At the Rex they were showing *The Guns of Navarone*; several hundred Parisians were queueing up for the 8 o'clock screening.

ROGER THIRAUD

It wasn't just the Middle Ages that weighed on the class and led to its listlessness. The first cold weather and the rain that darkened the old building had a lot to do with it, as did the heavy lunch served in the refectory of the Lycée Lamartine.

At the start of the lesson, Roger Thiraud wondered anxiously whether the cause of this lethargy might not lie in the content of his teaching. Since his wife had become pregnant, he had developed a passion for the history of childhood, and his thinking on this topic would frequently be brought into his lessons.

Who has ever given a thought to the status of the wet nurse in the thirteenth century? No one! Yet, it seemed to him that research of this kind was worth just as much as those undertaken by dozens of eminent specialists on events as decisive as the circulation of bronze coinage in the Aquitaine Basin, or the changing shape of the halberd in Bas-Poitou.

He coughed and went on.

— After the period of natural lactation (he didn't dare say the word 'breast' in front of his pupils) it was not unusual in the thirteenth century, once the baby's first teeth came through, to see the wet nurse chew the food before slipping it into the child's mouth.

All twenty-two pupils suddenly came to life and noisily showed their disgust for such repugnant habits. Roger Thiraud allowed them to let off some steam, then he struck the blackboard with the edge of his ruler.

— Hubert, come here. Come up here and write down the titles of the following books which you must all, and I mean ALL, look up in the school library. Firstly, *De Proprietatibus rerum* by Bartholomeus Anglicus, chapter six, which will have the advantage of further improving your acquaintance with the Latin language. Secondly, the *Confessions* of Guibert de Nogent. The lesson is over. We meet again on Friday at three.

The classroom emptied except for a young boy who was having twice-weekly private tuition in Latin. The boy lived in place du Caire; they had got into the habit of walking up the Faubourg Poissonnière together, chatting about the day's events. Before they got as far as the boulevards, Roger Thiraud used the excuse of a trip to the delicatessen to take leave of the boy. He turned into rue Bergère, hurried round the block housing the *Humanité* newspaper building and was back on the boulevard. He caught sight of his pupil, two hundred metres ahead, running straight through the flow of traffic. He walked in this direction until he reached the frontage of the Midi-Minuit cinema.

Furtively, he entered the foyer, paid for his ticket and went into the darkened auditorium. He handed his ticket to the usherette along with a twenty-centime coin. The film had started; he would have to wait until the start of the next screening to find out the title.

Every week, on Tuesday or Wednesday, these two hours of dream-time made up for the effort necessary because of who he was to take the plunge and take his seat here in this place of perdition.

He had no trouble imagining his colleagues' indignation if they had found out that Monsieur Thiraud — you know the young Latin and History teacher whose wife is expecting a child — was in the habit of going to cinemas where they show films unworthy of a rational intellect.

How could he make them understand his passion for horror. None of them read Lovecraft! They might just about have heard of Edgar Allan Poe. As for Boris Karloff and Donna Lee in *The Body Snatcher....* The film lasted barely an hour and a quarter; he left the cinema with the director's name stuck in his mind. Wise, Robert Wise. A film-maker to look out for.

He wavered between the Tabac du Matin and the self-service in the basement of the *Humanité* building. There he could get a cup of coffee, take it to a table on a tray, and while he was enjoying the scalding liquid, he could have the pleasure of spotting the newspaper's famous bylines as they went past; the most illustrious names in the Communist Party. Thorez, Duclos, even Aragon came here for a break between meetings or while they were waiting for an article to be set.

Unfortunately, this evening he was running late; he made do with a drink standing up at the bar in the Tabac. *Le Monde*'s lead stories were the problems with the Franco-German treaty and the persistent rumours doing the rounds at the Twenty-Second Congress in Moscow.

Before crossing the boulevard Bonne-Nouvelle under the illuminations advertising the Water Wonderland at the Rex, he bought a bouquet of mimosa and two pastries. He thought of the day when he would have to buy three, and smiled. Lost in his musings, he nearly got run over by two young people, a boy and a girl hunched on an orange moped.

Now he had only to climb the fifteen steps of the rue Notre-Dame de Bonne-Nouvelle to be home. Without thinking, he glanced over towards the metro, just as he used to a few years earlier when he was waiting for Muriel. At that very moment, two Algerians emerged, their collars turned up against the wind. The time on Roger Thiraud's watch was 7.25 pm, on Tuesday, 17 October 1961.

KAÏRA GUELANINE

The two sheep started back in fright when the moped left the path and came to a standstill at the edge of the patch of ground that served as their pasture. Aounit kept it ticking over, revving the engine from time to time. He raised the index and second fingers of his free hand to his lips and gave a long whistle, then he waved the young boy over.

— You'll have to come back at once, dad needs you in the shop.

— What about my sheep?

— Don't worry, they won't stray! What do you think they'd do . . . dive into the Seine? Come on, jump on behind me.

The child got on to the seat of the Flandria, jammed the edge of his heels against the hub-bolts of the rear wheel and clung on to the saddle frame. Aounit rode fast. He would veer suddenly to avoid troughs of water and muddy surfaces. While this seemed to demand total concentration, he still managed to carry on a conversation with his brother.

— I'm going to Paris this evening with Kaïra. The trouble is, there are still three animals to be got ready for the Latrèche boy's wedding. Is there school tomorrow?

— No, the teacher's sick, and you know, on Tuesday nights there's my game. And the thing is, we're playing the team from avenue de la République.

— On the Pensioners' Cemetery ground?

— No, at the Swallows. The thing is, they're playing on home ground! It's going to be tough. If I don't turn up, they'll put the El Oued kid in goal. They might as well have a couscoussière.

— 'Sieve' is what the French would say.

— Why, do you think El Oued's French?

At Ile Fleurie the moped turned on to the tow-path so as to skirt the Papeteries Réunies warehouses. A chilly fog began to settle, bringing rain with it. It was already blanking out the top of the gasworks.

They sped into the shanty-town along rue des Prés. Twice, the noise of the engine backfiring attracted a swarm of kids all determined to climb on to the back. Aounit slowed down and headed for one of the few concrete huts. A man was carrying a skinned sheep's carcass over his shoulder. With his foot, he pushed open the door where the word BUTCHER'S was chalked in capital letters.

The window did duty as a counter; in the street two customers were waiting to be served. Near them, two men were busy patching up the roof of a hovel, nailing pieces of rubber cut from old tyres across the joins between the wooden boards.

Aounit wheeled his Flandria into the shop, went through the room and out into an interior courtyard. It was five years since his father had bought hut 247 for 300,000 old francs paid to a Gèmar family going back home. In those days, in 1956, they had only had three rooms and the courtyard. The shop, the parents' bedroom — where the youngest children slept too — and the room he shared with his brother and Kaïra. Later, he and his father had built two extra rooms, which meant his elder sister could have more privacy.

Kaïra was waiting for him in the courtyard. She was different from the other young women in the shanty-town. At twenty-five, all her friends had been married for years and had a bunch of kids in tow. This courtyard, or one just like it, would be their whole universe; that and the Prisunic at Nanterre. A horizon of waste ground squeezed between the factories and the Seine, ten minutes bus ride from the Champs Elysées! Kaïra knew women who hadn't set foot outside the shanty-town for two, even three years.

Her mother had been like that. The day she died, Kaïra had vowed she wouldn't just live as other people thought a woman should. She took care of her brothers and sisters, seeing to it that six people's daily needs were met. Shopping, cooking, overseeing schooling, housework, laundry and repairs, wood and coal supplies; and on top of all this, the drudgery of fetching water. Those buckets that had to be filled in all weathers from the well in the square, and stored in the courtyard for the cooking, the washing, the toilet, the shop . . .

She kept her vow, and the reverse side of this accepted submission to the good of others was that she freed herself, imperceptibly, from the burden of tradition. This slow process of alteration was marked by what the neighbourhood perceived as sudden acts of daring unimaginable for a 'real Algerian woman'.

Kaïra remembered how jittery she'd been the first morning she'd ventured out wearing trousers. Not jeans, like her brothers wore, but loose terylene that hid the shape of her body as well as a dress did. Nobody had gone so far as to comment out loud when she went by, hardly so much as a few smiles, quickly frozen by her stare. She could keep no check on her pride; she would rather have died than admit it had taken her weeks of practice at home before she could face being judged by others.

Holding a glass, she went up to her brother.

— Here, drink this, it's orangeade. So you've decided to come with us?

— I'm keeping to what I've told you. I'm happy to go with you as far as your meeting-place, then I'm straight off to the Club. Tonight The Wild Cats are playing on Albert Reisner's programme. Missing the beginning is bad enough.

— If it's too much trouble to give me a lift, I'll go by bus and metro.

Aounit put his arms around Kaïra and gave her a little kiss on the cheek.

— You get unusually touchy whenever your boy-friend comes up ...

She wriggled free of the hug, taking refuge in the kitchen.

— Think whatever you like! To be in Paris by 7.30 on public transport I'd have to leave right now. I still have to meet people from other parts of Nanterre, to say nothing of which the couscous isn't ready. You won't be putting yourself out to feed the children.

— Forget what I said, I was only teasing you. What time will it be over?

— I don't know, 10 or 11, but don't worry, Saïd and Lounès will bring me home. They've arranged things with a friend of theirs who lives in rue de la Garenne near the Simca workshops. Tomorrow morning they'll take the circle bus from Porte Maillot as far as La Villette. Lounès has left his car there.

— It would be easier for you all to go together and get the car tonight. That would save them trouble of bothering the guy at la Garenne.

— You may be right, but we have a plan to follow. We'll be a lot safer in the metro than in a car after what we've got in store for them!

All the time she was talking Kaïra was kneading the couscous and breaking up the lumps of semolina between her fingers. She spooned some eggs into a saucepan of boiling water, then set the table for the children. She took three Vitho yoghourts out of the screened larder on the wall.

— You can tell father everything's ready.

She left the house, greeting her father's customers in the street. She headed for the Water Board houses. For some unknown reason the Water Board had left this as waste ground, with four abandoned buildings, crude red-brick blocks like big rectangular boxes. A number of families had moved in and had extended their dwelling areas by building another storey out of corrugated iron and planks of wood. As months and years went by, other families had joined them and now the buildings formed the heart, the radial point, of a conglomeration of huts and shanties where five thousand people lived: the Prés shanty-town, the shanty-town of the meadows.

Before she climbed upstairs, Kaïra struck a match to light the ramshackle steps. Three women and a man were waiting for her in a sparsely furnished room. They got up when she came in, each in turn greeting her and making the motion of the hand to the heart and the forehead.

— We haven't got much time, so listen carefully. Our initial target is the Neuilly bridge. At five to eight you are to meet the people from Bezons, Sartrouville and Puteaux on the Dion Bouton embankment, opposite the Lebaudy gardens. The people from Colombes, Courbevoie and Asnières will be on the other side of the bridge, on the Paul Doumer embankment, up by the Ile de la Grande Jatte. To get to Neuilly you must go through Puteaux avoiding the main thoroughfares. And make sure you go nowhere near Mont Valérien, it's full of cops. I'd say the safest route is via rue Carnot and the Bas-Rogers, towards the old cemetery. Once you're there, you're to wait quietly until five to eight, when you're to go up on to the Neuilly bridge. Kémal and his men will be there; they'll tell you what's been decided.

She got up to go, but the man held her back by the sleeve of her sweater.

— Kaïra, you can tell us, there's no longer any need to keep it secret. Where are we headed? The Champs Elysées?

— Who knows? Maybe we're going to dechristen l'Etoile and call it the square of the Star and Crescent!

Aounit was waiting patiently at the end of the road. She ran towards him picking her way on tiptoe across the puddles of water and mud. She pulled a scarf tight over her hair, got on to the moped behind her brother and gripped him round the waist. They crossed the Nanterre streets, deserted because of the rain. On the way she recognised the gravel pit with its conveyor chute and, just after the allotments, the water tower perched on its four concrete feet. Three days before, a team had come from the transit camp and in broad daylight had ventured to scale the building so as to add

to the three white-painted letters O.A.S.* an I and an S
that turned the water store into an OASIS. They entered
Paris by the Puteaux bridge and cut into avenue Foch
across the Parc de Bagatelle and the Bois de Boulogne.
Day in day out Aounit drove through the city for a small
delivery firm; he confidently skirted those junctions
that were thickest with early evening traffic. The more
his sister begged him to take care, the more he would
rev the engine. He went through an amber light at the
last crossing on boulevard Bonne-Nouvelle and almost
ran over an inattentive pedestrian; a man with his arms
full of flowers and a box of cakes. Kaïra let out a
scream.

— Stop, Aounit, we've arrived. Saïd is waiting for me
at the metro exit outside a photographer's studio. Come
with me, just to say hello.

Aounit attached his moped to a no-parking sign; they
went on up the boulevard for some twenty or thirty
metres. There was nobody outside the Lily of the Valley
studio yet, but they had to slow down a bit because
walking just ahead of them was the man they'd very
nearly knocked down. Fortunately, he took a right
turning into a street that ended in steps. Just then Kaïra
made out Saïd's face coming out of the metro. Her
heart raced; despite the cold, she could feel her cheeks
burning. She took a deep breath to stop herself from
rushing towards him.

On the façade of the jeweller's shop at the corner of
rue Notre-Dame de Bonne-Nouvelle, the imposing
clock with the copper pendulum showed it was 7.25
pm, on 17 October 1961.

* Organisation Armée Secrète: the right-wing terrorist organisation
opposing Algerian independence.

CHAPTER TWO

At that very moment the shrill sound of a whistle was heard above the noise of the traffic and the hubbub of the crowd gathered on the pavements.

Hundreds of Arabs who'd been scattered in cafés, in front of shop windows and in neighbouring streets, answered the signal and invaded the road. Within minutes the demonstration was organised. Makeshift placards came out from under overcoats and in the distance someone unfurled a banner: No Curfew. A group of traditionally dressed Algerian women moved to the front, setting up those whooping calls known to the French as the you-you. Keeping up these calls, they flourished their gold-threaded headscarves. Other demonstrators waiting down in the metro came to join in. There were now more than a thousand Algerians blocking the Bonne-Nouvelle crossroads.

The owner of the Madeleine-Bastille brasserie was no stranger to public disorder. The plate-glass window on the corner had been smashed in twice before. The first time was in 1956 during an attack on *l'Humanité*, in protest against the Soviet intervention in Hungary. The second was in May 1958, during some demonstration or other, pro or anti de Gaulle; he couldn't remember which. With the help of the bartenders and a dozen regulars, he took in chairs and tables, then started sticking wide strips of paper across the inside of the windows, a technique well tried and tested during bombing raids. Better prepared, the newspaper office opposite lowered a metal shutter on its frontage.

Intrigued by the noise, Roger Thiraud turned back down the steps of the alley. He saw a huge crowd of Arabs going by and could clearly make out the slogan being loudly shouted just three metres away; Algeria for the Algerians.

So, they'd done it! The war whose only reality for most French people was a series of bulletins, alternately flat or triumphant, was coming to life in the centre of Paris. The concierge came out of the building, having been interrupted in mid meal. He was holding a napkin.

— It's the last straw! They think they're in Algiers . . . I just hope the army shows up to clear these terrorists off my street.

— They're hardly that scarey. There are even women and children.

— You obviously don't read the papers. Looting and massacre is the way they do things. They use their harem girls and their kids to plant bombs. So if you want my opinion, no mercy.

Ill at ease, Roger Thiraud moved on. Saïd and his friends were outside the Rex. The queue to see *The Guns of Navarone* had disintegrated. Aounit was busy unlocking the safety chain of his Flandria. Five hundred metres further on, halfway to the Opéra, Captain Hernaud of the Third CRS Company received the order to disperse the demonstration forming in Bonne-Nouvelle. It was the job of the Second and Fourth Companies to reinforce the brigade of mobile Gendarmerie deployed around the Neuilly bridge where there were reports of significant numbers of 'Arab Frenchmen'. Other police detachments were heading towards Stalingrad, Gare de l'Est and Saint-Michel. The radio car kept up a barrage of instructions. *Break the movement, don't hesitate to use your weapons if the situation demands it. In a face to face encounter each man has the right to act as he thinks fit.*

The captain was hurrying his men into the midnight-blue Berliét vans.

— Don't forget to adjust your masks. We'll start with the canisters, but in this wind there's a good chance we'll get it blown right back in our faces.

The weapons truck was empty. Regulations allowed for only a quarter of a company's men to be armed at the start of an engagement. They were temporarily suspended. Even the four teargas grenade launchers and the eight light machine-guns had been handed out.

Captain Hernaud gave the signal to move; with headlights blazing and horns full on, the column went up boulevard Montmartre and boulevard Poissonnière, taking no heed of the one-way system. The lorries came to a halt at the crossroads with rue du Sentier. The CRS grouped under the Zurich Insurance sign while a dozen of them cleared the cars that separated them from the demonstrators. When they'd done this, the vans formed a barricade that completely obstructed the roadway. Meanwhile other police had taken up positions behind parked cars. From this makeshift cover they launched the first teargas canisters. But a strong gust of wind blew the gas back against the buildings, dispersing it in the air. The captain gave an order to stop firing; he regrouped his troops in front of the headlit lorries. The demonstrators hooted with laughter at the failure of the police offensive, but some of them were worried by the sight of this mass of soldiery, covered to the knees with shiny black leather, dark helmets ridged with a solid strip of gleaming metal, and those indecipherable faces behind their motor cyclists' goggles. The blinding beam of the headlights obliterated any clear view of their weapons. Naturally, they had those long wooden clubs, as thick as pickaxe handles and as long as brooms, and shorter weapons that glinted in the light.

Suddenly, letting out a long howl, the huge silhouette started moving. Slowly at first, then gaining speed with every stride. It seemed as if nothing could stop its momentum; the hammering of boots on the cobble-stones reinforced this sense of doom. In the front ranks the CRS men seemed gigantic, puffed out by the bulletproof waistcoats slipped over their leather coats. The Algerians didn't move, as if nailed to the spot in a daze. Within their ranks hesitation was palpable; it was already too late to organise a defence. This suddenly became clear to everyone. The crowd flowed back as one towards the Rex, which is where the clashes began. Rifle butts came down on bare heads shielded only by arms and hands. A policeman threw a woman to the ground giving her hard heavy kicks; he struck out at her over and over again before moving on. Another one was using a club on the stomach of a young boy with such force that the wood broke. He kept on, using the sharpest fragment. His victim held up his hands to shield himself, trying to catch at the wooden handle. He soon lost all control of his broken fingers.

There were bursts of gunfire outside the Neptuna swimming pool where a motor coach was parked. Inside the building, three policemen were taking careful aim at those trying to escape, and missing none of their targets. A red and cream Simca parked less than twenty metres away, with a large number of Arabs sheltering behind it, was riddled with bullets. People ran screaming in all directions. In their panic they collided with bodies fallen on café pavements among upturned tables, broken glasses and bloodstained clothes.

Kaïra and Saïd were there, directly under fire. Aounit

was lying on the pavement, face down, near his moped. Dead or wounded. The gunfire petered out: there was a silence broken by the agonised cries of the dying. Only a lull! The CRS regrouped their ranks and came back on the attack. In the confusion of the crowd Kaïra was thrust to the very front, to be confronted by a kind of demented robot with raised truncheon. A dreadful, total fear paralysed her and left her breathless; she could feel the blood draining away from her face. In spite of the cold, her goosepimpled flesh broke out in a sweat. She couldn't take her eyes off this appalling creature who was going to kill her. The hand came down sharply, but with enormous difficulty Saïd managed to place himself in front of her, shielding her with his body.

The brutality of the blow knocked both of them flat. The policeman kept up his attack on Saïd. In the end he got tired of it. Kaïra was afraid to make the smallest movement that might lead their attacker to suspect she was still alive. She thought Saïd, lying on top of her, was doing the same thing, right up to the moment when she recognised the acrid sticky liquid that was spreading across her coat. Her fear was as nothing compared with the tremendous pain that gripped every atom of her being. Screaming, she raised the corpse of her friend.

— Murderers! Murderers!

Two policemen seized hold of her and took her towards a Paris bus requisitioned to transport arrested demonstrators to the sports hall and the exhibition ground at the Porte de Versailles.

Only Lounès was unscathed. He was trying to scatter the crowd into the side streets that ran off the boulevards. Numerous passers-by lent a ready hand to the CRS as well as pointing out the nooks and crannies where men and women were hiding, stunned by the horror of it all.

It was nearly eight o'clock. On the embankment below the Neuilly bridge two vast columns made up of shanty-town dwellers from Nanterre, Argenteuil, Bezons, Courbevoie, moved off. FLN* leaders lined them up and marshalled the endless groups of people who came to join them. There were at least six thousand of them; the four lanes of the bridge didn't seem wide enough to accommodate the flow of the procession. They crossed the tip of Ile de Puteaux, beneath them, and entered Neuilly. Not one of them carried a weapon, not so much as a knife, or the tiniest stone in their pockets. Kémal and his men were keeping a check on doubtful individuals; they had expelled half a dozen young guys who were keen to make trouble. The aim of the demonstration was clear: to achieve the raising of the curfew imposed two weeks before on Arab French only, and at the same time to show the strength of the FLN presence in France.

The road was clear; in the distance they could make out the Arc de Triomphe, illuminated to mark the state visit of the Shah of Iran and Farah Diba. As was their custom, the women were at the front. You could even see prams with children round them. Who could have suspected that three hundred metres ahead, concealed by the darkness, a squad of the mobile Gendarmerie lay in wait, backed up by a hundred Harkis. At a range of fifty metres, without any warning, the machine-guns let fly their hail of bullets. Omar, a young boy of fifteen, was the first to fall. The shooting continued for three quarters of an hour.

•

Roger Thiraud was both fascinated and horrified by

* Front de Libération Nationale: Alegerian National Liberation Front

what was taking place in front of him. His attention was transfixed by the lifeless bodies of the demonstrators. One corpse in particular, with its frightful shattered head, its mouth a deathly streak of shadow, dripped coils of blood like liquid snakes. On the opposite pavement, the first arrivals at the Théâtre du Gymnase were threading their way towards the glass doors guarded by over a dozen staff. The manager was cursing the bad luck that now blighted the opening night of a new Leslie Stevens play. So far he had been able to keep Sophie Desmarets in the dark about the bloody events outside, so as to avoid upsetting her, but the 'friends' besieging the actress's dressing room would make sure these efforts were in vain.

— They were asking for it, said a passer-by. Roger Thiraud stared at him.

— But they need medical attention, they ought to be taken to hospital. They're all going to die!

— You don't imagine they show any mercy for our side, over there. And after all, they're the ones who fired first.

— No, don't say that. I've been here since the start, I was on my way home ... They were running for dear life, empty-handed. They were looking for somewhere to hide, to shield themselves when the police opened fire.

The man moved on, heaping abuse on him.

The theatre manager came down the main steps of the building and stopped a police officer.

— Come at once, there are at least fifty of them who've got in backstage and in the wings. Our first night starts in ten minutes, you must do something about it.

The officer formed a detachment that he positioned outside the entrance to the stagehands' quarters, and, with a gun in one hand, flung open the double doors. A score of frightened men with their hands on the backs of their necks emerged into the bright light. In the corridor behind them drinks were being laid out to celebrate the anticipated success of the play.

Roger Thiraud was on the verge of speaking out but he lost his nerve. Powerless, he looked on as a driver who'd been stopped in rue du Faubourg-Poissonnière was badly beaten for trying to hide one of the injured in the back of his car.

Across the road near the circular post office building at the corner of rue Mazagran the prisoners were being rounded up. Large numbers of buses had arrived and were being filled with hundreds of haggard Algerians trying unsuccessfully to dodge the truncheon blows being dealt by the CRS lined up in front of the platforms. It had taken the RATP only twenty minutes or so to disrupt normal services and earmark buses for the demonstrators' transportation. One driver was reading the *Parisien* while he waited for the order to leave. Roger Thiraud made a rough tally of the number of packed buses that passed him. Twelve. He reckoned the number of injured men standing crammed together came to more than a thousand.

A photographer went round with the police as they carried out the most brutal actions. At regular intervals the flare of the flash would light up some bloody scene or other.

Another man had been watching since the start of the demonstration. He hadn't moved once from his corner of the Gymnase Café. Although he was wearing a CRS uniform he didn't seem particularly interested in what his colleagues were doing and just made it his business to keep a close eye on the precise movements of Roger Thiraud. He decided the time had come and emerged from the shadows. He crossed the boulevard, unhurriedly making for rue Notre-Dame de Bonne-Nouvelle; impervious to the cold and the rain, he took off his heavy leather overcoat and slung it over his left arm. At the same time he pulled his helmet well down and made sure that his goggles were on properly. At the rue Thorel turning he stopped and took a Browning out of his holster. He had given a lot of thought to his choice of weapon. The 1935 model was still the most universally used service pistol; even today it accounted for the fame and success of the Herstal national armaments factory.

He released the clip with its thirteen rounds and snapped it back in against his palm. He was at home with this weapon; at twenty metres he could empty the contents of the magazine on to a ten centimetre target. After taking the Browning in his left hand, under the leather coat, he walked on. It wasn't his first time, but he couldn't stop himself from shaking and clenching his teeth. The hardest thing was to suppress this desire to run away, to leave things undone. Walk, keep going, stop thinking . . .

He could now make out Roger Thiraud's features and mentally ran through the photographs he had been given. The same broad forehead, the tortoiseshell spectacles, even the peculiar shirt with the buttoned-down collar.

As with his previous missions, it was all a matter of acting quickly, too quickly for him to know quite why he found himself to the left of the schoolteacher. The very slightest of his movements was ineluctably connected to the completion of his mission. Nothing could stop him. It was as if he had gone beyond the point of no return. For a fraction of a second his right hand was hidden under the leather, then it reappeared clenching the pistol butt. Roger Thiraud paid no attention and the man took this chance to get right behind him. With a sharp movement he caught his head in an armlock. The coat flapped over the school-teacher's face as he dropped his bouquet of flowers and the parcel of cakes. He clutched at his assailant's hand in a desperate attempt to make him let go. But, with precision, the man put the barrel of the gun to Roger Thiraud's right temple, put his index finger to the trigger and squeezed it. He pushed the body forward and stepped back. The schoolteacher collapsed on the pavement, his skull shattered.

Calmly, the man put his gun away, put on his coat and disappeared up the steps of rue Notre-Dame de Bonne-Nouvelle.

·

At dawn on the boulevards there remained only thousands of shoes, small objects, assorted debris that bore witness to the violence of the clashes. Silence had at last taken over. A medical team sent by Police Headquarters was seeking out the injured and the corpses. They worked functionally and without moral scruples. The bodies were piled up in an undifferentiated heap.

— Hey, over here, this is the fifteenth stiff up here. Not a pretty sight, he got it right in the head! So, are you going to give me a hand?

— Oh shit, it's not a darkie! It looks like a Frenchman.

The leader of the team was in a bit of a quandary about his discovery; he decided not to take any chances and let his superior know at once.

The next day, Wednesday, 18 October 1961, the lead story in the papers was the railway and bus strike over wage increases. Only *Paris Jour* devoted most of its front page to the events of the previous night:

ALGERIANS TAKE OVER PARIS FOR THREE HOURS

Around noon, the Préfecture released its figures, giving three dead (one of them a European), sixty-four injured and 11,538 arrests.

CHAPTER THREE

At his mother's request, Bernard turned off the television. The presenter of the one o'clock news fused into a dot of light and disappeared.

— You can do it with the remote control, Mum, we got this model specially, so that you don't need to get up. You only have to press the buttons . . .

Muriel Thiraud only shook her head; she went on staring at the television, which sent back the darkened reflection of the room and of her own face.

She hardly ever left this armchair; in it, twenty years earlier, she had learned of her husband's death. Only the child swelling her belly had stopped her then from taking her own life. As soon as Bernard came into the world, she lost interest in him and lived like a recluse in the three rooms at rue Notre-Dame de Bonne-Nouvelle. She never went near the window, so as not to see, three floors below, the steps where one morning in October 1961, the body of her husband was found.

Bernard Thiraud was brought up by his grandparents; as a teenager he took to the study of history with a natural enthusiasm. During a conference on 'The Fears of the West', he had met Claudine Chenet; at that time she was starting work on a thesis whose topic, the working-class periphery of Paris in 1930, was an excuse for innumerable walks.

— You know very well that she can't get used to these gadgets, Bernard. We had better go. If we wait another hour, the motorway will be jammed. I can't stand getting stuck in slow-moving traffic . . .

Bernard went over to his mother and kissed her.

— We'll be back in a month. The beginning of September at the latest. I've left our address and our Morocco phone number with the concierge. If there's any problem, don't think twice about calling us; I mean, give us a week. We have to stop in Toulouse for a day or two and then we have to get across Spain.

Claudine shook hands with her future mother-in-law. They left the apartment without a flicker of movement from Muriel Thiraud. On the stairs Claudine couldn't refrain from saying:

— I'll never get used to it! It feels like talking to a ghost.

Bernard's only answer was to put his arm round her. The car, a pale blue VW, was parked near rue Saint-Denis. Claudine took the wheel and headed across Paris in the direction of Saint-Cloud. She slipped into the flow of holiday traffic. After the tunnel, she opened the roof and turned on the radio.

There were some hold-ups before they got to the Monthléry exit, mostly because of campers and trucks. Claudine was speeding along in the fast lane. Around seven they made a stop at Pons, 'biscuit city', then headed on towards Bordeaux. They spent the night at the Hôtel de la Presse at the Dijeaux gate, not far from the Garonne river.

The next day, they had to stop on the A61 between Damazan and Lavardac. Every time they braked, the Beetle veered off to the right. Bernard tried to make light of it.

— What do you expect from a German car? They always take over.

It only needed some tuning, and they reached Toulouse in time for lunch at Vanel's: cassolette of snails with walnuts, and a Cahors coq au vin.

— This is something to remember when we're trying to make the best of Moroccan cuisine.

— None of your culinary imperialism, Bernard, you don't know what you're talking about. I càn promise you some pleasant surprises.

— I can't wait to get there. I don't think it'll take me more than two days here. A few files to look up this afternoon at the town hall and tomorrow all day at the Préfecture.

— You still won't tell me what you're looking for?

He took a Gitane out of the pack and lit it before answering, tongue in cheek.

— No, it's a dangerous business I'm involved in, a mysterious organisation lurking in the shadows. I'd rather you knew nothing, for your own safety.

They left the restaurant. Claudine got into the car and drove to Occitane Square, just beside Saint Jérôme's. She went into the hotel. Bernard crossed the old town, heading for the town hall. He went through the public gardens to the Capitole. The pavement cafés were busy; he resisted the temptation to have a drink. He entered the town hall. In the entrance, a receptionist gave him directions to the archives. At 5.30 he was told they were about to close.

— So how's the big-time investigation going? Claudine asked him while he was taking a shower.

— I've got a lead . . . I'll know for sure tomorrow perhaps, at the Préfecture. On the other hand, I did find out something interesting. Just think that forty-two years ago it was here in Toulouse that the War Council of the Seventeenth Regional Command pronounced judgement and the death sentence on a certain Charles de Gaulle. On 7 July 1940.

— Send it into the papers, for the thousand-franc prize . . .

— Oh, clever. And what have you been doing?

— I've been waiting for you.

Laughing, she pushed him on to the bed.

Bernard Thiraud woke up very early. He arrived at the Préfecture well before the most punctual of its staff. He killed time standing at the bar of a café in the rue de Metz and came out as soon as the concierge arrived.

He was alone in the library. Now and then one of the staff would go by, arms laden with boxes, black registers, or else piles of magazines. The reading room stayed open all day; when he heard the nearby cathedral bells at noon he asked to use the phone. The receptionist at the Mercure answered and rang room number twelve.

— Claudine, this time I'm not joking. I'm really on to something. Don't expect me for lunch. The reading room closes at six o'clock, I think I'll work right through.

— I'm pleased for you. But don't be too late.

These were the last words they spoke to one another. At ten past six, Bernard Thiraud walked down the steps of the Préfecture and back up rue de Metz towards Place de l'Esquirol. A man sitting in a black Renault 30 got out from behind the wheel. He began trailing Bernard. Eager to tell Claudine what he had found out, Bernard was hurrying. He went up rue du Languedoc for a hundred metres, and turned right, round Saint Jérôme's church. After the busyness of the main shopping avenues, here were quiet streets and rows of private houses, some of them dilapidated, with high garden walls. Hardly any shops now, except for window displays of religious objects and antiques. Suddenly there was no one on the street, not even a car; Bernard became aware of the man who was following him. He turned, saw him two metres away fumbling in his pocket and taking out a gun. Bernard was curious, unfrightened by this breathless old man in his sixties; he looked around to see what could have made him bring out a gun. Before he could understand, the first bullet caught him in the shoulder, making him stagger. The gunman got closer, within touching distance. He could feel his breath. Bernard didn't have the strength to struggle, the second bullet went through his neck. He collapsed as his murderer emptied the last six rounds of the magazine into his back.

The man fled into the old town's labyrinth of small streets. Passers-by alerted by the gunfire found only the corpse of Bernard Thiraud lying on the pavement.

•

After six months in Lozère, at the Marjevols commissariat, after the repercussions of the Werbel affair, I got a transfer to a local station in Toulouse, in rue Carnot. Usually I ran the outfit as part of a team with Commissaire Matabiau, but he had first choice of holiday dates, and was taking it easy on some Corsican beach. It was the very time the gravediggers chose to take on their employer. A gravediggers' strike in the middle of a heatwave! There was no avoiding trouble and I found myself caught in the middle: on one side were the grief-stricken families, on the other the strikers. The Toulouse town hall refused to intervene and was playing up the public health issue. They had high hopes of public opinion being on their side, and couldn't give a damn about the police being caught in the middle. One morning in July brawling broke out between the gravediggers and the relatives of the deceased at the Rapas cemetery, near the mortuary where several dozen coffins were queueing up to be tucked away in a grave.

I positioned my men outside the doors of the cemetery cold store, where the workers, outnumbered and overwhelmed by the hysterical energy of the battling mourners, had taken refuge. At half past six we were still in among the graves.

One of the strikers tapped me on the shoulder.

— I'm going to try and talk to them, Inspector, to explain what's behind the action we're taking, if you can just calm them down. Their dead aren't at risk, we are guaranteeing minimum service . . .

The guy seemed convinced; used to wheeling corpses around, he failed to grasp that, for all their distress, the demonstrators facing him were none the less alive.

— Just stay where you are, and if you've got the key to this building, double lock it. What do you really expect? I'll try and reason with them.

He had never heard anything so astonishing.

— A cop as our spokesman!!! You're joking?

— It's not exactly my style. But I don't think a cemetery is the right place for settling scores. It's not up to them to sort out your problems, and the police have even less to do with it. So there's nothing to be gained by prolonging this farce.

— We're only asking for a dirty job allowance, like the sewer workers. When the old guys used to do exhumations there was nothing to worry about; they'd open the box and there'd be ten kilos of powdered bones. Nowadays we're digging up bodies from the sixties. The golden age of plastic . . . I don't need to draw you a picture, but we don't see too many bones! Stuff like that doesn't help you sleep at night. Nearly half the guys they take on leave after two or three days. They'd rather starve than make five thousand francs in those conditions. A three-hundred franc allowance is hardly asking for the moon!

A uniformed officer interrupted our conversation.

— Inspector Cadin, Sergeant Lardenne wants you to go to the radio car. He's had a call from headquarters about a murder in the Saint Jérôme district.

The gravedigger was genuinely put out.

— Another family on our hands!

I crossed the cemetery. The car was parked near the gate of the paupers' section, an area overrun with brambles, and with six or seven iron crosses knocked sideways. On a small heap of freshly disturbed ground stood a white porcelain vase with some flowers.

I pushed the gate open . . . Sergeant Lardenne, slouched on the front passenger seat of the Renault 16, was busy solving the mystery of 43, 252, 003, 274, 489, 856, 000 possible combinations of his Rubik cube.

— Well, have you done it?

He sat up straight and pushed the toy into his pocket.

— One and a half sides, Inspector, then I get stuck. My son can do it with his eyes closed; they do competitions in his class, eleven-year-olds.

— That's very interesting. Anything else?

He turned the same red as the Rubik cube.

— Yes, I mean, no, some passers-by found the body of a young guy. Shot dead with either a revolver or a pistol. Bourrassol's team is on the spot, it's right next to rue du Languedoc.

— Take the wheel, we're on our way. Turn the siren on, otherwise with all these holiday drivers we won't get there before dark.

Staff-sergeant Bourrassol knew his job; the different procedures called for in a criminal case were already under way.

— Inspector Cadin, I'm glad to see you. I've left the

body as it was found; nothing's been touched while we were waiting for you.

— Very good, Bourrassol. And your preliminary findings . . .?

— Very little. No eye witnesses. Ten local residents heard the firing. One of them saw a figure disappearing in the direction of rue de Metz, that's all. So we're still just poking around. He took something like ten bullets in the back, I'd say with a 9mm Parabellum. I've got his papers, definitely a tourist passing through.

In support of this claim he handed me a French passport and a brown leather wallet. The ID was in the name of Bernard Thiraud, student born in Paris on 20 December 1961, his address given as 5 rue Notre-Dame de Bonne-Nouvelle in the second *arrondissement*. A Paris University student card and several photographs, all of the same young woman, were inside the transparent sections of the wallet. The wallet pocket contained eight thousand francs in travellers cheques and a bill from Vanel's for two, the evening before.

— At least he'll have no regrets about his last meal. Four hundred and thirty francs for two! Bourrassol, get on to whoever was holding the other knife and fork. And give the sewage works a ring; tell them to check the outlets within a radius of a hundred and fifty metres. You never know, maybe the killer got rid of his weapon nearby.

— It's not easy, Inspector. They persistently refuse to give us any help at the sewers . . .

— Those people think they're above the law. What's more, they get a special allowance, not like the grave-diggers!

— What do you mean, Inspector Cadin?

— Just thinking aloud. Forget about the sewer people, I'll take care of it.

The next morning, at nine o'clock, the city's Director of Technical Services came into my office and handed over a plastic bag containing a weapon.

— There you are, Inspector, you only have to ask. A council worker fished it out of a duct in rue Croix Baragnon. The current isn't very fast there . . .

— We can deduce then that the place where it was found roughly corresponds to the place the murderer chose to throw away his pistol.

— Is it a pistol? I've never been really clear about the difference between a revolver and a pistol.

— Elementary, they have different mechanisms. Pistol-magazine and revolver-cylinder. Your man hasn't touched it, has he? They were told exactly what to do.

I held the gun by the barrel, without taking it out of the protective bag, and took a look at it.

— We're dealing with a professional.

My interlocutor didn't hide his astonishment. He must have been brought up on Conan Doyle and Richard Freeman.

— How can you tell?

I explained, at the risk of shattering his nascent admiration for me.

— What we've got here is a Llama Especial No. 11. A pistol as widely used as our Unique L. It counts for nothing that there are fifty of them per square metre; each gun has particular characteristics and laboratories have the resources to decipher them. The problem with the Llama Especial is that it's manufactured in Gabilondo, in Vitoria. If you happen to know that this factory is located in the province of Guipuzcoa, right in the Basque country, you'll begin to understand.

— Not in the slightest . . .

— In 1972 an ETA unit attacked a lorry loaded with this kind of gun. Three hundred pistols disappeared. We don't know how they got them but now and again the French underworld uses pieces from this job. We regularly come across weapons with their reference numbers. We check on the list drawn up by the Spanish police and they match. That's all we need; it takes us straight to the Vitoria factory! The lab can then get on with looking for prints, but no one goes to the trouble of getting an untraceable pistol just to leave fingerprints on it ... Thanks all the same, it's something to be going on with.

He extended his hand, making a slight respectful bow. On the landing I couldn't resist unsettling him a little more.

— Thanks again, I'll do the same for you. If there's a crime that needs solving, whether it's personal or professional, don't think twice about getting in touch.

Sergeant Bourrassol was next to arrive in my office. I had never seen him perturbed or unsmiling. He wasn't like that, it seems, when he worked at headquarters in Mirail, the new town on the outskirts of Toulouse. He was accused of laying a heavy hand on two juvenile delinquents at the Narval, the café in the town centre.

— We had no trouble tracking down the lady. When they ate at Vanel's the night before last, they asked the owner to recommend a hotel. He sent them to the Mercure Saint-Georges, a hundred metres from the scene of the crime. We haven't told her anything, she's waiting for you. Or should we bring her here?

— No, let's go. Tell Lardenne to mind the shop and let him know where we'll be.

The hotel management could have done without our visit; I was asked to park the black and white car at the far end of the car park. For discretion's sake, we were ushered into a private salon.

Claudine Chenet had obviously had a sleepless night; she had heavy shadows under her eyes. When she saw us she got to her feet.

— What's happened to Bernard? I want to know . . .
I let out a long deep breath.

— He's dead, murdered. It happened last night, shortly after six, not far from the hotel.

Her features took on a look of utter weariness. I had to strain my ears to make out what she said; her voice was very faint.

— But why? Why?

— I'm here to find out, Mademoiselle. What time was it when he left you?

— Very early in the morning. I was still asleep; probably before eight. Check with reception. He was doing some research at the Préfecture and he rang me at noon to tell me he wasn't coming back for lunch.

— What kind of research?

— He didn't want to tell me; he just joked about it, pretending he was on the trail of some international organisation.

— Unfortunately it's possible that it wasn't a joke. Have you met anyone in Toulouse since the day before yesterday?

— No, Inspector, nobody. We were on our way to Morocco for a holiday. We made a detour to Toulouse, but it's the first time I've ever been here. Bernard too. The first and the last.

— Did you go out yesterday afternoon or in the evening?

She gave the rueful shadow of a smile.

— I suspected you'd get to that. The answer is no. I had lunch in the hotel restaurant, check with the waiters; crudités, tournedos, strawberries and cream. Then I read on the balcony, in the sun.

— And you weren't worried by his disappearance! Your boyfriend was due back at 6 pm and the next morning at half past eight my men find you eating croissants, with hardly a hair out of place. Forgive my surprise, Mademoiselle Chenet, we are dealing with a crime.

She raised her hands to her forehead and burst into tears.

— It often happened that he didn't come back at night. In Paris . . .

— Did you live together?

— Yes, we LIVED together, that's the right word. Bernard had been living with me for six months. Some nights when he was depressed he would disappear and come back in the early hours, with no explanation. His mother is to blame, I mean for his lack of self-confidence. When he was born his father had just died in bizarre circumstances. That's all I know about it, except that the death badly affected Bernard's mother. She never leaves her apartment, and in ten or so visits I've only heard her speak three times.

— All right. We're going to take away your boyfriend's personal belongings. Sergeant Bourrassol will give you a receipt. Of course, you must stay in Toulouse for a few days, to facilitate the investigation. The most painful part is still to come. You must come with me to the morgue, to identify the body before it goes for autopsy.

•

While we were away, a witness had turned up. Lardenne made him wait in the corridor, in front of the glass door of my office. He was between thirty-five and forty, wearing leather trousers, a multicoloured check jacket and a splendid pair of cowboy boots. A real jerk!

Gritting my teeth, I turned on Lardenne.

— Well done, it's carnival time. I hope for your sake that he won't be a waste of time.

Before pushing the door open I eyed my ageing

hipster; he had taken out a comb and was sliding it through his hair, sleeking it with his fingers. In the palm of one hand he curled a lock on to his forehead. I asked him to sit down.

— So, you have something to tell us about the murder of this young Parisian.

He threw his arms in the air, jerked his head back, and spoke in a squeaky high-pitched voice.

— That's going a bit far. I noticed this kid the other night when he came out of the Préfecture. Where I hang out is just across the road, Verdier's Bar. It's the only place you can play Pachinko.

Lardenne had no idea what he was in for when I'd finished with this clown.

— Well I never. And what exactly is Pachinko?

He seemed happy to find an interested beginner.

— A Japanese slot machine, a bit like pinball. You buy some little steel balls at the counter and you put them into a box that's hanging on the wall. You manoeuvre the balls round things. If you get to the target, you win some more balls . . .

— And then?

He looked at me in puzzlement . . .

— Well, after that, you start again!

— Terrific. Well go back and play with your little balls. I've better things to do than listen to you drivelling on.

— But Inspector, I really saw this kid, he wasn't alone. I gave a start.

— Not alone! What do you mean?

— Well, I'd finished my game and I was just leaving when the Parisian leaves the Préfecture. I get a kick out of watching nice-looking boys and I can't deny this one was easy on the eyes.

I was planning to follow him when I noticed that another man was on his tail. The guy was rolling in it, at any rate he was driving a black Renault 30TX . . .

— You saw his car. Can you remember the number?

— No, just the département, 75. Another Parisian. So I gave it a miss and treated myself to another go at Pachinko.

— Can you describe your rival, how tall, what he was wearing?

— He was about average height, maybe five nine, hair turning white, most of the time he had his back to me, but I'd say he was about sixty. He was dressed like an executive type, a grey suit, black shoes.

I called Lardenne.

— Thanks for this one, he's the first to have seen the murderer. He goes around in a black Renault 30TX registered in Paris. He must have been following Thiraud all the way here. Contact the gendarmerie, the highway police and all the toll-booths between Porte de Saint-Cloud and Sept Deniers. Drop everything else for now. There can't have been more than ten cars like this one on the Paris-Toulouse road over the last couple of days. Find out what speeding tickets have been issued. As for me, I'll make checks here in town; you never know . . .!

It was just gone eleven; I had already run up an interrogation, a visit to the morgue, and an interview with a Pachinko fan! I needed a good cup of coffee to help me digest it all. I strolled over to the drinks dispenser. I inserted my two coins forcefully. A plastic cup dropped down. A stream of brown water, broken by a few bubbles, filled it up noiselessly. A clear plastic stick dropped into the drink, bringing the process to a close. Sipping the coffee, I was rudely interrupted by shouts coming from the waiting room. The commotion went well beyond the usual level of hassle with the public. I went to the area behind the open counters. The officer on duty buttonholed me right away.

— We can't make sense of this. All these people have been summoned by Commissaire Matabiau, but we can find no trace of their files . . .

— How many are you dealing with?

— About thirty so far, Inspector; they keep on coming. If only the Commissaire had filled us in.

— I'll try and sort it out. Give me one of these summonses.

He handed me a sheet of blue paper, a standard form, telling the recipient to show up immediately. The reason was underlined as usual: Creation of new computer file: — anti-terrorism. The final paragraph explained why all these people had wasted no time getting there: *Those summoned are obliged to appear and be registered. Failure to do so is liable to a penalty of up to ten days imprisonment and 360 francs fine. (Articles 61, 62 and following of the Penal Code.)*

The official stamp, Commissariat Carnot-Toulouse, half covered the date of dispatch: 28 July 1982.

— Get the names of everybody who shows up with a summons like that, and tell them to go home and not to worry. They'll hear from us in a few days. I'm sure this is a hoax we're dealing with.

— How do you know, Inspector?

— You did the right thing sticking to office work . . . Matabiau went on holiday on 13 July, I don't see how he could have signed these papers the day before yesterday. Some little smart alec is winding us up, but it won't be too difficult to track him down; to start with draw up the list of staff who have access to the blank forms and official stamps. Sergeant Bourrassol will make an initial selection and send me the names of the lucky ones.

•

Three days later, there was only one problem solved:

Toulouse town hall awarded a 250 franc special payment to its gravediggers. There was a unanimous vote for a return to work. That let me lift the security cordon at Rapas cemetery and get back four men.

Nearly two hundred Toulouse residents had laid siege to the duty desk of the station, outraged that they should be suspected of terrorism, without me getting any nearer the source of the forgeries. The investigation into Bernard Thiraud's murder was marking time. The ballistics laboratory's report was languishing on a corner of my desk. A trial shot had been made with the weapon that had been found. The ballistic test result was a formality. This was clearly the pistol the murderer had used. The cartridge casings and the bullets were an identical match. The lab had been meticulous to the point of including an enlargement, thirty times actual size, of the markings on the bullets. The trajectories told me that Thiraud had received two bullets face on and six others in the back when on the ground; face on they were clean hits, the laboratory judged firing distance to be between two and four metres, while the next shots had left significant burn traces and the murderer could have been no more than half a metre away from the victim.

Sergeant Lardenne's report gave me nothing more to go on. It would have been easy to believe that the Renault 30 didn't exist, if the driver hadn't made the blunder of signalling its passage with a corpse.

— Have you questioned the petrol station attendants, Lardenne?

He raised his arms in the air and slapped them down on his thighs.

— Of course, Inspector. One thing at a time. It's not hard to work out, a car like that has a fifteen gallon tank . . . On the motorway you reckon it'll average twenty-five miles to the gallon. Assuming he filled it up to start with, he's sure to run dry somewhere around Marmande or Agen! In any case he must have had to stop for petrol. And yet, no service station dealt with this car. In either direction.

— Why do you think he'd have left Toulouse?

— It seems obvious. I'd say it was a contract job. The guy's supposed to wipe out Thiraud; once the job's done he goes home . . . Everything suggests we're dealing with a professional, the pistol he used for instance. A Llama Especial from the batch stolen in Spain.

— I agree about the gun, but there's something that doesn't fit . . .

— What, Inspector?

— The murder. Read the lab report. It's easy to reconstruct what happened. Thiraud is walking towards the killer. Everything suggests he doesn't know him. At a range of three or four metres, the guy takes the gun out and puts two bullets in him, one in the shoulder, the other in the neck. When Thiraud is on the ground he finishes him off with six bullets in the back at point blank range. Do you know many professionals who work like this? No! A hit man, an executioner would have waited for the target to come within a metre; he'd have reached forward and stuck the barrel on the heart, or on the temple, according to taste. One bullet, two at the most. Instead, our fellow empties the whole magazine, at the risk of waking up the neighbourhood and getting collared. Read this bit: only the lesions caused by the second bullet crossing the neck were fatal. None of the others hit a vital organ. Those six extra bullets make me think the murderer was directly involved; that would explain his zeal. He's not a professional, but an amateur who knows what he's about. They're the toughest. To get him we'll use up more energy and hard thinking than you need to solve a Rubik cube. Don't you agree, Lardenne?

I gave him no time to answer.

— Come on, we're making a visit to the Capitole. Before he died Thiraud looked up the archives in the town hall and the Préfecture. He was going to teach history; what he was doing probably had some connection with his studies. After all, nothing should be overlooked . . .

The car park in the market square was full. Lardenne found a spot in rue du Taur outside the Cave, a drinking club. We were out of luck: Prodis, the Deputy Mayor in charge of Public Information, was orating in the entrance hall of the Capitole as we made our way in. He abandoned his listeners and came to meet us.

— Inspector Cadin, Sergeant! What a coincidence, I was thinking of giving you a call . . .

He took my arm and led me behind a huge flower arrangement that acted as a screen.

— It can't happen again, Inspector, they must be stopped at once, or else they'll drag us in the mud . . . You too! The press knows nothing yet, but I can't count on it! As soon as they get a whiff of rotten meat they'll be fighting to get their teeth into it.

He was dripping sweat. Acrid waves of body odour hit my nostrils. I kept catching my breath so as to cut down the olfactory aggression.

— Arrest who? You'd better tell me! I promise you I'll do my best.

— The situationists!

— Who?

— The situationists. An organised gang that's sending out false summonses about the anti-terrorist files. We're getting hundreds of complaints on the phone. The Mayor's office is deluged with people wanting to complain. Don't forget he's also a Deputy and he plays a leading role in the Lower Chamber. They played the same trick in 1977 before the local elections, you must remember.

— In those days I was working in Strasbourg and I wasn't particularly interested in how elections were cooked up in Toulouse.

— You don't say. Excuse me, this business is driving everybody mad, all round the building they're talking about nothing else. In 1977, it was no joke: ten thousand copies of a fake town hall bulletin sent out, a phoney press conference, the national press going wild. Even a demonstration by the unemployed! The situationists simply announced the ending of welfare benefits for fifteen hundred unemployed; they were asking them to turn up and put in a claim for emergency needs at the town hall. At eleven in the morning the square was swarming with people and you'll never guess what they'd dreamt up! Three truck-loads from Pojol's, the city's top delicatessen. In the Mayor's name they'd ordered a luxury buffet for two hundred people: petit fours, smoked salmon, caviare, foie gras. I'll leave to your imagination the reaction of the unemployed, convinced they'd lost everything, when the waiters from Pojol's tried to mingle with trays full of snacks.

— Pretty smart. Did you get these situationists? You don't put your hands on files with fifteen hundred addresses without leaving some clues.

He shook his head and a few drops of cooled sweat spattered on my cheek, making me shiver in disgust.

— No, never. Though that campaign must have been costly. They disappeared, apparently gaining nothing from the campaign. Everybody was targeted, Baudis as well as Savary. Then not a thing for six years. A few months ago we thought we'd come up against them again with the CLOC.

I've always been a believer in giving a wide berth to town councillors, but Prodis's talents as a storyteller could easily change my mind. Having summoned up this mysterious organisation, he cut himself short, anticipating my question.

— Yes, the Committee for the Liberation and Organisation of Computers. A group of smart alecs who hacked into the regional computer centre. Because of them we had to re-do the forms for the local taxes! All the work went up in smoke. That lot is behind bars and we were able to establish that what they did was nothing to do with the situationists.

— I've got everything in hand to find these forgers; they won't be free for long, I can promise you. For the moment I've got a murder on my hands and you'll understand that that has to come first. It's preferable to have hoaxers at liberty than a murderer.

— Inspector, I don't share your opinion. Make your murderer wait, he'll be only too happy, but stop them from doing damage. They're trying to destabilise us, it's democracy that's at stake.

— I can only say again, we're dealing with this problem. And let me tell you now that I'm the one who decides priorities in my work. If you don't agree with me, take a trip to the morgue. Ask to see Bernard Thiraud, say I sent you!

I left him rooted to the spot and went back to Sergeant Lardenne. Next stop the archives! According to the department head, Bernard Thiraud had been interested in administrative documents to do with the years 1942 and 1943. He gave us a table and brought us all the files the victim had looked at. I glanced through the contents of one box: contracts, draft agreements, resolutions, a whole hotchpotch of papers covered in official stamps, dates and figures. Nothing out of the ordinary. If only we knew where to begin! The day promised to be difficult. It stayed that way. I found nothing significant, unless you count the 1942 tax on dogs for the Toulouse region.

Lardenne unearthed a wad of documents from the War Council condemning de Gaulle, who was a brigadier then, to the firing squad for high treason. At half past five, among the council workers, we left the Capitole, discouraged. Lardenne dragged me towards the Florida, a bar in the square.

— It's years since I've set foot in here. It was our meeting place when I was a student. I remember the rumour that you had to be careful what you said.

— Oh, why's that?

— It was the most cop-infested joint in Toulouse. A myth, of course . . .

— Come on then, for once it'll justify its reputation.

•

Next day, at the Préfecture, we were met by M. Lécussan, the Director of Administrative Archives, a wrinkled old functionary disabled by a club foot. He preceded us into the warren of stacks. His body wobbled to the left, but whenever his head looked like bumping into the metal uprights, he would straighten up with a thump of his orthopaedic shoe on the parquet floor. An almost inaudible grumbling accompanied his uneven gait.

— After your telephone communication, Inspector, I consulted the files that the victim wanted to study. The entire DE classification. The sort of old stuff there's so much of here. I've had all the documents placed in my office. You'll be more comfortable working there. I'm completely at your service.

He closed the door quietly then went off down the corridor with his lopsided rhythm.

— Useful that, we know he won't be listening at the door ...

Lardenne's joke cheered him up; he seized the first wad with enthusiasm.

DEforestation ... DEmarcation ... DEfence ...

The administrative papers that we looked at that day were little different from the previous ones. This time they concerned the whole of the Haute-Garonne département, not just the city of Toulouse. We were soon experts on sanitation problems in Muret and Saint-Gaudens or the complaints registered in the districts of Montastruc and Leguevin over road repairs to the N88 and N124 highways. The vagaries of filing mixed comedy with tragedy. A note from the Prefect demanded the annulment of the DEliberations of the special DElegation from Lanta, with the excuse that the members of the municipal council had met in the back room of the inn. The letters that followed showing their move as caused by the collapse of the town hall roof carried no weight and the Prefect stuck to his decision. The envelope file indexed after DEliberations bore a carefully hand-written inscription: DEportation.

DEportation was treated in exactly the same way as other administrative tasks. The bureaucrats seemed to have filled in these forms with the same punctilious-ness they brought to coal coupons or the new school year. Death was being allocated in place of hope. With no questions asked. Pinned to a cardboard file, a yellowing telegram signed Pierre Laval, dated 29 September 1942, advised the Prefectural authorities not to split up Jewish families marked down for deportation and noted that *'because of the strong feelings provoked by this barbaric measure, I've had an assurance from the German army that children won't be separated from their parents and can go with them'*.

A pile of circulars bearing the initials AV activated these directives.

Against barbarism, a trip to Buchenwald and Auschwitz!

I entrusted the file indexed DEployment to Sergeant Lardenne and plunged back into the bureaucratic maze of DElousing.

CHAPTER FOUR

The doorman at the Mercure was busy stowing suit-cases in the boot of the Beetle, while Claudine Chenet was settling the bill in reception. I stopped her as she left.

— Hello, I wanted to say goodbye before you left.

— I wasn't expecting such courtesy from the Toulouse police. You're doing your best but it won't make me like this city . . .

— I'm very sorry . . . I came to give you confirmation that Bernard Thiraud's body will be sent home on Monday. We didn't learn much from the autopsy.

At this reminder of the pathologist's role she closed her eyes for a long moment.

— I'm sorry, I can't get used . . . Do you have a lead?

— No, not really. We have a clear enough description of the presumed murderer. Sergeant Bourrassol is now drawing up a list of all the people who were in the Préfecture on the evening it happened. Then we'll check their movements, their financial situation, their love life . . .

— What for? What can that have to do with Bernard's death?

— Listen, it's just a wild hypothesis, but it has to be allowed for: let's suppose that the murderer only has an approximate description of his target and that your friend matches this description . . .

— No, that can't be! That would mean that Bernard died for nothing. Just somebody's blunder, nothing more!

— I've already said it's just a working hypothesis but it's impossible for me to overlook it. The murderer and those who hired him, if this is the case, must have realised their mistake. The one thing on their minds will be to carry out their contract. My job consists in preventing them. I'm all too familiar with wild goose chases . . . But don't worry, it doesn't mean I'm giving up the first lead. It's very likely that the murderer did carry out his mission. That would imply that he was on your trail in Paris, or that he knew about your departure and destination, and came straight here.

— You seem to have it all worked out, Inspector.

— Otherwise, I can't understand why a murderer would come to Toulouse to kill a man he has on the spot in Paris! He then found out where your hotel was and he trailed Bernard the morning he went to the Préfecture. He watched him all day, then followed Bernard when he left. He took advantage of a quiet street to commit his crime.

— But how was he able to locate us so quickly?

— At first sight that looks complicated. But when you're looking for someone and you're determined to get hold of them, you realise it's no big deal. Your relatives and friends knew about your plans. The murderer made a phone call passing himself off as a close friend. Where do we go from there? In just the same sort of way! As for your hotel, it's child's play. The tourist office publishes an annual guide to Toulouse hotels. All the guy had to do was note all the numbers and call each one until he reached the letter M for Mercure Saint-Georges. When he asked, the receptionist was happy to confirm that Monsieur and Madame Thiraud were staying there. The hotel has 170 rooms, the switchboard handles an average of 1,200 calls a day. I got the figure from the management. Unfortunately, no one remembers so inconsequential a call. Which is not surprising.

The doorman of the Mercure had finished loading the luggage and came over to us. Claudine didn't notice him. I took twenty francs from my pocket and slid them into the palm of the liveried guy's hand. He thanked me with a forced smile and an exaggerated bow. Claudine realised and tried to pay me back.

— No, keep the money. How about this? I have to spend a few days in Paris for the investigation. If you'll give me a lift . . . I'll keep you company on the journey.

She agreed without a second thought. I joined Lardenne, who was waiting in the hotel car park, and interrupted his struggle with the Rubik cube.

— Pass me my case. I'm not taking the train, Mademoiselle Chenet has suggested I travel with her. The return is as planned, pick me up next Saturday off the eleven o'clock train.

— Okay boss, so long as you don't find another driver to bring you back!

When I thought about it, it was the very first time he'd called me boss.

•

We had passed Blagnac airport on our left. The Volkswagen's speedometer was steady at a hundred and thirty. At this rate we would arrive in Paris by mid-afternoon. But when she saw the service area at Saint-André de Cubzac, she decided to make a stop. It didn't bother me. Even the greenish transparencies recommending the incomparable flavours of the dishes served at the bar didn't manage to spoil my appetite. A Spanish tourist bus emptied its load at the door as soon as we'd sat down. I ordered egg mayonnaise and grilled meat with chips. Claudine made do with crudités and tea. Apart from formalities (You don't mind if I smoke? You're not getting a draught?) she hadn't uttered a word since we left Toulouse. I tried to get the conversation going again.

— What's your field of study?

I was taken aback by the brusqueness of her answer.

— History.

I allowed myself ten mouthfuls of reflection before venturing a new question.

— Which period? My efforts were rewarded; she emerged from her melancholy.

— The Paris outskirts in the early part of this century. More particularly, the population that settled on the site of the fortifications of Paris, after their demolition in 1920. Roughly where the ring road is today.

The reminder of her research had enlivened her; I decided to stay on the same ground.

— That's a funny subject for a young woman like you! I've read a few of Auguste Le Breton's books; it seems more like a retired army man, even a cop, who'd be interested in this kind of subject. Bernard was a historian too. He specialised in the Second World War, I belive?

She put her down her fork and stared at me, frowning a little.

— No, not at all. He was preparing a thesis on childhood in the Middle Ages. Your information is incorrect.

— It was only a guess! At the Capitole and the Préfecture your friend consulted files of documents on the period 1942/1943. I concluded that he was taking advantage of your trip to Toulouse to check archives that were unavailable in Paris.

She asked the waiter for two coffees, then sat with her face resting on her upturned hands, her cheeks squeezed between them. Her long varnished nails made sharp points under her eyes. I took a good look at her for the first time; something I'd been unconsciously avoiding was now forced on me. These few moments of intimacy bought us much closer, Claudine was no longer just a client. I'd known she had to leave the city that morning. The examining magistrate had told me and the first thing on my mind had been to get that order sending me to Paris . . . In my brief career I had twice before fallen in love with witnesses or victims. And to think some people see the police as heartless! First in Alsace, where I'd met Michèle Shelton, the girlfriend of a murdered young ecology activist. Then in Courvilliers, a dormitory suburb of Paris. There too I'd been slow to admit my interest in Monique Werbel. There was good reason; when I made her acquaintance she was stretched out on her bed, a nine-millimetre bullet lodged in her chest. Even a third-rate psycho-analyst could get ten years of fortnightly sessions out of a no-hoper with that on his mind. Eros and Thanatos, cursed as always.

I hadn't taken my eyes off her.

— Why are you looking at me like that, Inspector? You're making me uneasy, as if I was under suspicion.

— Do you want me to be honest?

— It's your job to be, I think. Otherwise, who are we to believe in!

— I'm stricken with an occupational disease that's very common among young cops, especially when they're face to face with a witness as pretty as you.

Her hands dropped; she sprang to her feet.

— Stop this at once, Inspector. I'm not driving you to Paris to hear this kind of thing, but to help the investigation. I don't have it in me to play the indignant

widow, and given that I'm burying Bernard this week,
I've got quite enough trouble to cope with.

The next words she said were in the Saint-Cloud
tunnel, five hundred and fifty kilometres later.

— Where can I drop you?

— At the corner of avenue de Versailles, there's a taxi
rank.

She didn't suggest taking me any further and her car
screeched through first gear after leaving me on the
pavement.

•

Next day, my first visit took me to the Ile de la Cité. I had
to show my clearance five or six times over before
being shown the central files. Having satisfied the last
usher, I went into the room on the fourth floor.
Everything was grey; the floor, the walls, the shelves.
Even the staff in their dark overalls, with hair and faces
that had taken on the dominant hue. A warm dusty
smell hung over the vast room. An old smell matured by
long years, imprisoned by the wide curtains at the
windows and the succession of double doors that led to
the stairs.

A note pinned up at the entrance told me that the
system of classification depended on two different
pieces of data: the surname of the person sought and
the presumed permanent address. I handed my request
to the man at the desk. With a jerk of his head he
pointed to a free chair. I sat down next to a police
bureaucrat defeated by the thanklessness of his task.
The search took an hour; I was called to the window
and given a brown card.

A) Alphabetical file: Bernard Thiraud. Not listed.

B) File by arrondissement: 5 rue Notre-Dame de

Bonne-Nouvelle, Paris 2. Files for 1. Alfred Drouet. 2. Jean Valette. 3. Roger Thiraud. 4. Françoise Tissot.

I filled out a form for Roger Thiraud and gave it to the attendant. He was back right away and wrote down the details in front of me.

A) Alphabetical file: Roger Thiraud, history teacher at the Lycée Lamartine, born 17 July 1929 at Drancy (Seine). Died 17 October 1961 during the FLN disturbances in Paris. A European probably connected to the Algerian terrorist movement.

The registry office at the town hall confirmed that he was indeed the father of Bernard Thiraud. I rushed over to Police Intelligence. A colleague I'd been a student with in Strasbourg had been made head of the ID section. By a stroke of luck he was in his office, buried in the glossy contours of a magazine for the modern man.

— How are things, Dalbois! You've got things easy in this department! Does the boss have it delivered?

He started, leaving the magazine open at the centre-fold.

— Cadin, what a surprise! I thought you were in Toulouse. What are you up to in this part of the world?

— Don't worry, it's all above board. I'm working on a murder case; a Parisian who got himself shot just round the corner from my headquarters. That gets me eight days in Paris on the expense account. And what about you?

He made a gesture that suggested ups and downs.

— So so . . . We're weeding out files. We have to hand over everything even remotely to do with terrorism to the new department they've set up at the ministry. That's all I've been doing for two months now. No more field work, they've turned me into an office worker!

He got up and unfolded his long frame. From a side

view the lack of exercise was plain: a roll of fat circled his waist and stretched the fabric of his summer shirt. He still had the yellow complexion of people who don't tolerate alcohol but can't do without it. In five years he'd lost most of his hair; the baldness gave way to a thin border that began just above each ear and spread out on the nape of the neck. He still dressed with care, although his modest salary compelled him to shop for chainstore clothes, rather than at Pierre Cardin.

— If it's not on business, then are you just paying me a visit in memory of the good old days? Though I remember we didn't always see eye to eye!

I went over to him and touched him on the shoulder; it was a friendly gesture.

— We never had a fight ... The fact is, I need you to put me in the picture about something that goes back more than twenty years. To October 1961 to be exact.

— What's that got to do with your investigation?

I decided to be straight with him. He hadn't been given this job because of a pretty face. At the least sign of fudging he'd clam up for good.

— The father of the guy killed in Toulouse died during the Algerian disturbances of 17 October 1961. I found that out from the file. It may be a lead. You've heard of the bagmen, the Europeans that collected money for the FLN and laundered it through Switzerland ...

He nodded and sat forward in his armchair.

— Yes, of course. The Jeanson network and the whole shebang ... There are still two or three old-timers here who followed the affair from start to finish. All the channels stopped operating in July 1962 with independence. The files are classified, buried. I think that even all the French sentenced for having helped the FLN have been amnestied. I can't see what you expect to uncover there, except trouble for yourself.

The efforts he was making to convince me had quite the opposite effect. The area was too sensitive; 'childhood friend' had turned into guard dog.

— Let's suppose Thiraud senior got mixed up in the FLN's laundering operations. His liquidation in October '61 could be the work of undercover men with the job of cleaning up the political landscape ... In those days, Frenchmen who went over to the other side weren't much appreciated.

— That's going a bit far, Cadin, do you realise what you're saying?

— Yes, absolutely. Early on, a few cases came to court but it was counter-productive. It gave them good publicity and made martyrs of them. Don't tell me that you work in this service without being aware of these little details. They've always operated like this. To liquidate the OAS too — it was a former prefect of Seine-Saint-Denis who ran the Gaullist commandos. Anyway, it's only an idea about the undercover guys, I'm not ruling out the possibility that the FLN was responsible, for example, a reprisal for the disappearance of a package or a punishment for a messenger who talked. I'd even say I find this explanation more satisfactory, since it has the advantage of connecting with the son's murder. Suppose he was nosing about in his father's affairs and discovered some of the FLN's war treasure...

— Just now when you came in you had a go because I was glancing at a bit of soft porn. You're happier with melodrama! Where's your war treasure stashed? In a secret room in the Capitole?

— Maybe in Toulouse. It's one of the cities with the biggest number of ex-Algerian colonists, people with a tendency to live in the past. It's worth checking out! I'm only asking you for one thing, to get out Roger Thiraud's file so that I can see what's in it.

He snatched the black telephone sitting on the corner of his desk and dialled an internal number with three digits.

— I'll see what I can do for you.

The number he wanted was clearly engaged since he had to try twice again before getting through.

— Hello, Gerbet? It's Dalbois in ID. I need something on the bagmen. It's possible that some of them recycled themselves into the terrorist networks. You must have a report to hand. While I'm on the subject, throw in the file on Roger Thiraud, an FLN character, a European. He died in the Algerian demonstrations of October 1961.

He hung up, pleased with himself. He seemed happy most of all because he'd shown the extent of his power to an inspector from the provinces.

— You'll have all that in fifteen minutes. By the way, are you married?

— No, I don't have the time to get settled with all these transfers! We'll see in Toulouse . . . And you?

He patted his belly and looked up.

— Isn't it obvious? You must meet Giselle, she's an excellent cook. What about tomorrow night? I'll arrange for my mother-in-law to babysit the two kids.

I thought it would be wise to accept. At least I wouldn't have to entertain the kids. One of Dalbois' colleagues, it had to be Gerbet, came into the room and put a hefty file on the desk.

— There you are . . . That's everything we have on the aid networks to the *fellouzes*. You may be getting in deep, there are several names in red on the terrorist list. They get taken out once or twice a year! Especially the ones who moved in Burdiel's circle. But I warn you, they're very big fish, no one's ever managed to prove anything . . . It's all a matter of things fitting together, coincidences, then we're in the dark. Even when

Burdiel got himself shot by the Honour and Police group, there was still no evidence.

As he was talking, the guy kept giving me little sidelong looks. Dalbois decided to put his mind at rest.

— He's a friend, Inspector Cadin. He's investigating some murder or other in Toulouse. He's taking the opportunity of a trip to Paris to look up old buddies! You can go on, Gerbet, it's just between ourselves.

Gerbet shook my hand and went on talking to Dalbois.

— If you do stick your nose in there, be careful. They executed Burdiel after some dirty tricks inside our own ranks. When the Algerian war ended he gave up active service and became an advocate of rapprochement between the Palestinians and the Israeli left. We were conned into believing he was in touch with armed elements, operating in France, and that his apartment was a stash for arms. There were deliberate leaks from the investigation files and the press took up the story. A week later Burdiel was taken out by the Honour and Police group.

— Okay. I'll watch my step. And the Thiraud file?

Gerbet placed a buff-coloured file in front of Dalbois and opened it. It contained three or four typewritten sheets.

— I can't imagine what you can want with this character. You can sum up his life in two lines . . .

Dalbois grabbed the papers and snapped at him:

— I don't give a damn about his life, what interests me about him is his death! Leave this stuff with me and I'll get it back to you before tonight.

Gerbet left the room, bidding me goodbye.

— Charming guy your colleague. I thought things would be less relaxed in an intelligence section. You only have to ask nicely and you get home delivery of state secrets.

— Not by any stretch of the imagination. Some are uncooperative, but not Gerbet. He can't refuse me.

— And why's that?

— Just between us, my job consists in knowing everything there is to know about a great many people. As a rule, things they themselves are keeping quiet. Imagine for a moment that you work at the Préfecture and there are persistent rumours concerning the moral integrity of your wife ... for instance that she's partial to the company of very young girls ...

— Couldn't happen, I've already told you I'm not married!

Dalbois smiled.

— That's not how it is with Gerbet. Let's not talk any more about all this. Otherwise I'll look like a bastard. Let's check your man's pedigree ...

He took a card out of the folder.

— Roger Thiraud, born 17 July 1929 in Drancy, Seine, died 17 October 1961 in Paris, Seine. History teacher at the Lycée Lamartine, Paris. Married Muriel Labord. One child born after father's death (Bernard Thiraud 20 December 1961 in Paris). Resident at 5 rue Notre-Dame de Bonne-Nouvelle, Paris second *arrondissement.* No political or trade union involvement. Member of the Society of Historians. In 1950 his name appears on a list of signatures referred to as the Stockholm Appeal.

— What was this Appeal?

Dalbois put down a sheet of paper and looked at me.

— An international petition to ban atomic weapons.

— Was that the Communists?

— They were involved, but the Appeal was signed by more than a million French people ... If you go through it you come across half of the deputies on both sides of the house. You can't attach too much importance to connections of that kind. There's also the forensic report: *Found dead from a bullet in the head, right temple, following the Algerian riots on 17 October 1961. Likely time of death: between 7 pm and midnight. Autopsy: none. Clothes and items found on the body: wool three-piece suit, with Hudson label, size 42, grey, white pinstripes. Pale blue shirt, size 38. White vest and underpants with no label. Black Woodline shoes, re-soled. Black socks, Stemm label. Difor watch, still going: wallet containing identity card and professional card from the Ministry of Education in the name of Roger Thiraud. A bill for 1,498 new francs for a Ribet-Desjardins television set with two channels. One hundred and twenty-three new francs in cash. A cinema ticket from the Midi-Minuit cinema.* That's all. Your customer's not giving much away!

— No. I couldn't care less whether he wore Petit Bateau underpants or Eminence . . . The only thing I find worth knowing is that he went to a cinema called Midi-Minuit. Do you know it?

— By repute; these days they've turned it into a porno hall, but at the time it was the rendez-vous of horror film fans. They featured vampire and witchcraft films. At that time it was as much frowned on to visit this cinema as it was to spend an evening in Pigalle.

— If my name was Hercule Poirot, I'd note down the ticket number and be off to the National Cinema Centre to check the precise date this ticket was sold. Once I've got that sewn up I can find out the title of the last film Roger Thiraud saw. And the usherette's age into the bargain. What more can I ask? Nothing. This file is incomplete. Or worse, it's been doctored. There must be more hard info . . . This demonstration, for instance. I found out some things. The Préfecture acknowledged between four and six dead, depending on press releases. The police union published figures confirming sixty dead. While the League for the Rights of Man . . .

When he heard these words Dalbois clenched his right fist and mimed the motion of sticking a finger up an imaginary arse.

— Yes, I know what you think of this kind of organisation, but in this particular case their view is worth as much as anyone's. They talk about two hundred dead on the evening of the disturbances and as many again during the following week. The point I'm trying to make is that we're talking about something big here. An Oradour massacre in the middle of Paris; nobody knows anything about it! A slaughter on this scale has to leave traces . . .

Dalbois scratched his cheek and leant back in his chair.

— I'll see what I can do.

He lifted the telephone and rang Gerbet.

— I've just taken a look at these papers; it's pretty thin. As soon as you're free come and pick them up. Anyway, I've one or two more questions for you.

He turned to me.

— He's coming straight down. Let me take care of this. And keep playing the country cousin; you do it so well!

Two minutes later Gerbet was sitting on my right, listening to Dalbois, who was waving the buff file in front of him.

— You have to admit it's pretty amazing, a history teacher gets picked up off a Paris pavement with his head stuffed with lead and no one bothers with an autopsy. Nothing. No inquiry either; no search either for the causes of death or the murderer! Incredible! According to these papers there was no connection established between Roger Thiraud and the FLN. He seems like a quiet little guy, just a harmless teacher.

What's behind it? There has to be more to it. Are you in the know?

Gerbet shifted uneasily in his chair. He cleared his throat.

— Listen, Dalbois, leave well alone. It's twenty years since anybody poked about in this business. It would be no help to anyone now to demonstrate that a history teacher was working for a subversive organisation and that the French state decided to get rid of him. These days there are two countries with an interest in what happened then: France and Algeria. There are certain ghosts both governments would prefer not to bring back to life. The discovery of the Kenchela graves was proof of that. Labourers unearthed more than nine hundred skeletons when they were building a football stadium in the eastern Aurès. Everything pointed to them being soldiers in Boumédienne's army executed by the Foreign Legion. It had a camp on the same site. The Algerian authorities didn't make a fuss about it. They just used it for domestic purposes. There was no anti-French campaign unleashed as a result. It took a muckraker from *Libération* to do that.

— You mean we'll have to wait for *Libération* to tell us the reasons for Roger Thiraud's death?

— That's not what I mean at all! Let's be clear about this. The people in power in France nowadays condemned what the police did at the time. The great majority of them. If the past was dug up it would only create tensions with the Algerian government. Old quarrels and resentments would be revived. It's time to forget, if not forgive.

— I don't get your drift, Gerbet. If those in charge nowadays criticised the police and the role they were made to play, it would suit them very well to bring out the file and get all worked up about it as a way of showing how principled they are.

Gerbet didn't seem to appreciate the turn the conversation was taking. He wriggled even more and had now gone back to giving me worried looks.

— To be honest, the General Services Inspectorate carried out an inquiry in October 1961, under pressure from the opposition. A bit like Begin and the Sabra and Chatila massacres. Seven judges were placed under the authority of the then Minister of the Interior. You must know that this guy is now President of the Constitutional Council, which gives you an idea of how careful we have to be before re-opening the case . . . Among other things the judges had to give a verdict on the cause of death of sixty people whose bodies had been taken to the Institute for Forensics the day after the demonstration. Roger Thiraud's body must have been in the same bunch. Another coincidence, that Commission saw the light of day thanks to the insistence of the present Minister of the Interior.

— And the outcome?

— 'No further action.' In the report's conclusions it was established that the Paris police had done their job, which was to protect the capital from a riot started by a terrorist organisation. Very little was made public. The work of the Commission and a summary of those groups involved that night are contained in two volumes. One is at the Ministry, the other one is here in the police archives.

Dalbois rose to his feet smiling.

— Well now, that's the one I want to take a look at.

Gerbet had turned very pale; he was sweating profusely. He had sunk into his chair, his shoulders hunched forward.

— It's out of the question. Nobody can get at it. Only the Minister has the authority to have it taken out of the safe and to make its contents known. You know the law about publishing state papers. Fifty years of total secrecy. It's not in my power to rescind it. And there are some files so explosive they'll rot for centuries before they see the light. You know as well as me that governments need a strong united police force. Exposing what happened in October 1961 would have the opposite effect. The decisions of a Minister for the Interior and the actions of a Prefect of Police would be under scrutiny immediately. That kind of upset would provoke the destabilisation of a good half of the CRS units. They are still under the command of the same officers. Who would want that kind of upheaval? Certainly not the politicos. What they'd gain would be small compensation for the loss of confidence throughout the army and security forces.

Dalbois decided to let him off the hook.

— What's really great about you guys in Intelligence is the way you really know all the files … Don't worry, Gerbet, I'm not going to ask you to divulge state secrets. Especially since it's our job to manufacture them! If I'm reading you clearly, the ground is all marked out. One mistake and I've blown it. At least I know where I am. You really don't have any sources I can use?

— Sorry, there's no easy way. It's back to basic police work. Go through the newspapers for 1961, leaflets, informers' statements. We've got a good collection on microfilm, as well as a few thousand police pictures. But nothing specific. There were some problems with the police photographer, Marc Rosner. He was supposed to cover the Special Brigade's action, but he never delivered the films, at least that's the official version. At the start of the 60s amateur film and photography wasn't as widespread as today. We've only got a dozen shots or so taken by bystanders. Apart from that it was established that a Belgian television crew from RTBF made a fifty-minute film. They were in Paris to cover the official visit of the Shah of Iran and Farah Dibah, but they filmed the demonstration, first from their car, then from a café. Belgian television didn't transmit it, that was their only concession ... We tried unsuccessfully to buy the reels from them. I can tell you how to locate Rosner and the Belgian film people ...

I interrupted.

— For Marc Rosner there's no need; I came across him on another case.

Open-mouthed, Dalbois shot me a dirty look. Gerbet now stood facing him.

— What's this? Whose investigation is this? ... On what authority should I be helping this gentleman?

Dalbois told him about the leads I was following on the murders of Bernard Thiraud and his father. He just about managed to calm down his colleague, promising to keep him posted. As soon as the office door was closed, Dalbois bawled me out.

— I take the trouble to extract all the information we can get from one of the top guys here with some delicacy, and all the thanks I get is that you land me in it. Deliberately ... That's what it looks like. I understand why you don't manage to stay long in the same posting. Getting rid of a big mouth like you is a security measure! Anyway, tell me how you got to know this Rosner, I'm interested.

— It was last year, in Courvilliers. A murky story of faked photographs meant to compromise local bigshots. By chance I came across Marc Rosner. He was the technical knowhow behind it. His legitimate business can't have been bringing in enough money.

— Why, doesn't he work for us any more?

— Not since 1961. A guy from the Identification section told me about the bother he'd had with his superiors. Rosner was a bit weird, he liked messing about with corpses after the lab guy had gone ...

— You don't mean ...

Dalbois looked genuinely horrified.

— No, all he did was adjust the poses, set up a kind of still life. It didn't do any harm and it had no effect on his work. Everybody closed their eyes to it except the Director of the Prefect's office who'd made up his mind to have Rosner's neck. In September he'd been given two warnings and the head of Identification had been called up . . . Rosner was on duty the evening of the demonstration; he probably got all the most violent stuff on film. I've been told about Algerians impaled on the railings of the overhead metro, rapes in the police stations. With all this Rosner believed he had an ace up his sleeve and thought the boss might be more under-standing. He boasted about it with some colleagues. A few days later a break-in team did over the Préfecture photography lab and Rosner's home. All his files and archives were taken. Rosner found himself on the street, sacked for grave misconduct. He then opened a studio in Courvilliers: photojournalism, weddings, first communions.

— That's what you can look forward to if you keep on sticking your nose in.

— I haven't a clue about photography!

— Then you'll be a private detective. By the way, don't forget that you're coming to my house for dinner tomorrow evening.

•

In the lift I was already working on finding a way out of his invitation. I didn't need to meet Giselle Dalbois to know what she was like. The little not too distant suburb, French-village style, the pebbledash bungalow with adjoining garage, all amenities. When Dalbois had talked about me getting married, his pat on the stomach had summed up his own marriage with an economy of gesture. Madame Dalbois was no more than that: a well-heaped table. I couldn't see how an evening of boredom would alter that opinion. I walked as far as Saint-Michel metro and got into a taxi with dilapidated seats. An alsatian was asleep on the seat in front of me. Its eyes kept flickering open and its body shuddered in nervous spasms. I fumbled in my pocket, but as soon as I took out the cigarette pack the animal started growling. His master gave voice.

— He doesn't much like people smoking in his cab. I'm the same. Where to?

— Courvilliers, rue de la Gare. It's after Aulnay-Sous-Bois.

— That's one hell of a way.

He turned on his digital display meter. I became absorbed in watching the red figures change, being particularly impressed by the way five would turn to six, or eight to nine, with a single stroke. At regular intervals the driver would try to strike up conversation on the relative faults of Arabs and Africans. In despair at my silence he made a stab at anti-Semitism, with no more success. Out of steam, he took to whistling Serge Lama's latest hits.

As we reached the Exhibition Park the dog stood up in its seat and shook itself, at once filling the car with grey-and-tan-coloured hairs. The driver gave his animal an affectionate pat that managed to settle him. The car left the motorway heading round the huge workshops of the Hotch factory, then made towards the station.

— We're here. That's sixty-two francs, plus twenty francs for the return.

I groped in my pockets and gave him the exact amount.

— The last of the big spenders! Who's the tip for?

I leant towards his window and dusted down my jacket and trousers.

— For the dry cleaners! I'll be needing it to pay the bill . . .

The taxi shot off with the brakes screeching. As it turned towards the motorway turn-off I could still hear the driver shouting and the dog barking.

CHAPTER FIVE

The photography studio looked no different from the year before. I pushed the door open; a bell announced my arrival to a young woman busy refilling a drawer with fresh film. She turned and asked what she could do for me. She had a perfectly shaped face, with soft, regular features. A few very pale freckles on her cheekbones and under her eyes echoed the colour of her hair. But the harmonious modulation of her voice wasn't enough to disguise the nervousness that went with her pronounced stammer.

— C . . . can I h . . . help y . . . you?

— I'm Inspector Cadin. I've come to see Monsieur Rosner. Does he still work here?

She forced herself to answer. I clenched my teeth and my fists to stop myself from telling her to write it down and end the ordeal.

— M . . . my fa . . . father is doing a phot . . . photo story on the ex . . . ex . . . park for the town hall.

— Thank you, tell him I'll be waiting for him in the Bar des Amis.

The photographer joined me half an hour later, the same as ever, in the same black corduroy suit that was worn away at the knees, with a Leica slung over his shoulder. He seemed in a good mood.

— This is a surprise, Inspector! I could hardly believe

my daughter. You're coming back to us?

— No, I have a posting in Toulouse. I'm on a case that's a bit out of the ordinary. By coincidence your name came up in connection with some goings-on to do with this business.

He leaned closer; without saying a word he motioned to me to go on. I summarised the Thiraud file.

— And what do you think I can do for you, Inspector?

— I'd like you to tell me what you remember about October '61. Especially if you went anywhere near the Faubourg Poissonnière. I won't involve you in my report, you have my word. I only want to understand what really happened that night. Nobody wants to talk about it, there's very little evidence left . . . If Bernard Thiraud hadn't died in Toulouse, I'd probably still be in the dark.

Rosner fell back in his chair and began to rock.

— Where will stirring up the past get you, Inspector? You're surely not expecting me to give you the murderer's name just by sifting my memories. I got through more than ten rolls of film that night, three hundred and fifty frames at the very least! I don't remember shooting a single European face, apart from the cops.

— Were there dead among the security forces?

— No, not one, not even injured. But some CRS asked me to take them in hunting poses, one foot on the body of an Algerian . . . When I think about it that really surprised me. The demonstrators were unarmed; at no point did they try and organise to fight back. At best they tried to run or take cover in doorways. Everything contradicted the information given out by the liaison office. At the start of the troubles the police coordination section, a kind of crisis unit set up at the Préfecture, was talking about a dozen cops shot by the FLN at the Madeleine and the Champs Elysées. I got down there right away with a busload of reserve militia. They were roaring mad when they heard the radio ... Like wild animals. We got there and there was nothing! We asked around; none of our guys had so much as a scratch. From then on, though, it was hell for the Algerians. Within fifteen minutes I counted six corpses ... To say nothing of the injured. From the Madeleine I went down to the Opéra. The whole area was a battlefield. I recall one scene, a group of demonstrators pursued by the CRS had piled into the Café de la Paix, on boulevard des Capucines. The cops didn't even have to go in and get them, the staff and customers threw the fugitives out and saved them the trouble. It comes back to me bit by bit ... Just before that I'd stopped opposite Olympia to photograph arrested demonstrators being rounded up. I can see the concert poster ... A Jacques Brel concert. It was in one of my shots. A bit later a bike cop took me up boulevard des Italiens, to Richelieu-Drouot. A score of buses from the Third CRS company were set to go up to République. I stayed with the action.

— Still on the motorbike?

— No, in one of the buses. They were armed to the teeth! Rifles, tear gas launchers, hand guns, not counting the truncheons. They all wanted their pictures taken before they got down to it. A good number had served in Algeria; the driver had commanded a DOP in Oran province.

— He'd commanded what?

— A Detachment for Operational Protection! Fifteen or twenty squaddies who had the job of keeping tabs on a small geographical area, and making contacts with the locals ... Gradually, their mission was narrowed down to dismantling the aid networks to the Resistance, any way they could. There was a lot of talk about torture with electric shocks, but that wasn't the worst of it. Having the soles of your feet burned with a blowlamp took a bit of doing! Ah, DOP! In those days they'd give it out on the way into the swimming pools... Don't you remember that, Inspector? Little individual sachets of DOP. Hair washing, brainwashing.

To get back to your evening, they set up a barricade with their lorries, just behind the Rex cinema, and they got down to shooting. I took cover in the foyer of the Midi-Minuit. I'll always remember the name of the film they were showing that night: *The Body Snatcher*, with Boris Karloff and Bela Lugosi.

— I won't need to go to the Film Institute.

Marc Rosner didn't go on; he signalled to the café owner to serve us two more coffees.

— Oh, why's that?

— Roger Thiraud probably watched a film in that cinema before he was killed. At any rate, he had a ticket for the Midi-Minuit on him when he was found dead.

— I can't see why anyone should have planted a cinema ticket in his pocket. There's no law against history teachers being keen on horror films. For my own part I did the job I was supposed to do there, one eye glued to the viewfinder. I'll tell you something, photography counts for a lot, even at the time. You don't really see what's happening, just light, crowds, framing. The photographer isn't a witness; it's his film that plays that role. The moment you press the button, you fix an image without knowing what it contains. You know that photo a reporter took in Salvador, photographing the soldier pointing a gun at him? He released the shutter at the very moment the soldier pressed the trigger; he must have known his life was on the line, but it didn't enter into his considerations. The lens was a screen. It's possible that I photographed your man's murder, but what's certain is that I didn't see it.

— Don't put yourself out, Rosner, I'm well aware that

you might not want to help me. You're under no
obligation.

— You're wrong, Inspector, I'm not backing off.
October 17 is an important date for me. It marks the
end of my career as a cop. You may laugh, but I really
liked that work! It's twenty years since I've talked about
it to anybody. I promised myself I'd put it behind me.
Today you land on me out of the blue; you make me
unburden myself of stuff that really matters to me.
Give me time to clear my head. I think I crossed rue du
Faubourg Poissonnière, just where *l'Humanité* is. I had
a coffee in the Gymnase bar. There was a Belgian
television crew there. They couldn't believe their eyes.
They have to make do with rumbles between Flemings
and Walloons. They'd taken cover behind the jukebox.
The cameraman was shooting non-stop. I'd say they
can't have got anything special, it was dark; they could
hardly have set up a barrage of floodlights and turned
them on the cops! I was working with flash. After the
café I went next door to the theatre. There were CRS
clearing out a bunch of Algerians who'd managed to
get backstage. I stayed there until nine to take a bit of a
breather. The manager gave me a glass of champagne;
they were celebrating the opening of a play and he
must have taken me for one of the paparazzi.

— You noticed nothing on the other side of the
boulevard, near rue Notre-Dame de Bonne-Nouvelle?

— Nothing . . . I'm sorry, Inspector. When I left the
theatre I went straight to the Exhibition Park at Porte
de Versailles where they were rounding up the arrested
demonstrators. The Préfecture couldn't find a sports
ground that was big enough or near enough. It wouldn't
have suited them to lock up prisoners of war in the
Colombes football stadium! To cut a long story short,
there was shooting from all sides at Bonne-Nouvelle.
That's where they counted the greatest number of dead

and injured, apart from the lock-up yard on the Cité.

— You mean to say that demonstrators died inside the Préfecture? That's impossible, they'd never have managed to break in.

— No, there was nothing impossible during that night of madness. The government acknowledged three or four dead . . . A figure that ought to be multiplied fifty-fold at least, to get near the truth. A team from the Institute of Forensic Medicine was called around two o'clock in the morning on 18 October, to take delivery of forty-eight corpses, in a single bunch, in the small park that was next to Notre-Dame before work started on the underground carpark. Not a single one of them had been killed by a bullet. The diagnosis was the same for them all: clubbed to death. There was persistent rumours that they were FLN leaders who had been transferred to the Cité for interrogation. They were under surveillance in a first-floor room, when a dozen cops walked in with sub-machine guns raised. The prisoners thought their time had come; they rushed for the door at the back of the room and it gave way under pressure. It so happened that this door led directly into the main office of the Prefect. Shooting was out of the question. The Prefect and his entourage coordinating the operations heard the stampede. Their first thought was that this was an FLN attack on the central command. The entire guard of the Cité was unleashed on the prisoners. Result, 48:0. A nice score. Next to figures like that today's police 'errors' are quite modest! I'm telling you all this, Inspector, even though it never happened officially. No proof. No trace of those forty-eight bodies: the Institute came up with a cut and dried explanation for each death. They all ended up in history's dungeons. Don't think of bringing them to the surface; they'll be like Dracula, it'll be your blood that'll bring them to life.

For the first time Rosner had dropped his customary ironic posture. He pulled himself to his feet with his hands leaning on the table.

— You have the knack of getting your nose into the thickest shit, Inspector, but you don't get yourself out by stirring it . . .

— How then?

— By dropping others in it.

*

I got back to Paris on the RER train, arriving at Gare du Nord just before five. There were only a few passengers, hurrying towards the bus stops. I crossed the shopping arcade and came out on the forecourt. The square was grey and empty. A red-haired young woman was walking in front of me; with half an eye I watched the way her legs moved. Each step stretched the fabric of her skirt and I could see the line of her panties, faint but still strikingly visible. I was eyeing her so intently that the woman turned and looked me up and down, directing a long challenging stare at my crotch. She was wearing a T-shirt with the name Natalie printed on it. She moved off towards the Gare de l'Est.

It occurred to me to pay a visit to Madame Thiraud but I decided against it. It seemed more polite to ask if we could meet, letting her decide on a time and place. Leaning on the bar at the Ville de Bruxelles, I was about to order a Gueuse when I was gripped by an idea. Opening my notebook, I asked the waiter to call a number in Belgium for me. Five minutes later the switchboard operator at Radio Télévision Belge Francophone was finding out just what I wanted.

— I'd like to speak to M. Deril or else M. Teerlock in the News and Documentary section. It's about a film made for the Nine Millions programme.

— It's nearly ten years since that programme went off the air. It ended in '73. Our population's gone over the ten million mark ... M. Teerlock retired last year, but I can put you in touch with M. Deril. He's in charge of news features for the evening slot.

I didn't want to hear the history of the news programme, so I cut the conversation short; I got Jean Deril's extension.

— Hello, Inspector Cadin of Toulouse speaking. I'm investigating the death of a young lad whose father died during the disturbances of October 1961 in Paris. We don't have much documentation in France, at least accessible documentation. I'd like to view the films that you made at the time ...

— This is unexpected. Especially from a policeman ... Over the last twenty years, I've learnt how little interest these documents had for the French courts. I'm glad to put them at your disposal. We can fix a date.

— Well, the thing is I'm at the Gare du Nord. The next train for Brussels leaves at 5.45. I can meet you any time after eight this evening.

— I appreciate the company of decisive men, Inspector. That's fine by me. But don't come to the TV studios on boulevard Reyers, I won't be here then. We're filming a sequence at the fleamarket on Jeu de Balle square, a two-minute taxi ride from the station. You won't miss us, there'll be three location buses as well as the director's car. What is it exactly that you want to view? Teerlock made a ten-minute film with edited footage and commentary that was never transmitted. Your ambassador must have had something to do with it! Otherwise we kept all the footage unedited in the archives, about an hour of film with no sound.

— I'm not interested in the edited version. I'll be happy with the material shot as it was. See you later then at the fleamarket.

There's nothing better than a frontier crossing to make you feel you've embarked on an adventure. Cambrai, Valenciennes, Mons! I was really looking forward to this Belgian outing. The last one had been two years ago. . . . I was working in Hazebrouck then, in a state of deep despair, and more often than I should have done I would end up in a sleazy bar that closed at dawn. On one of these depressive evenings I'd bet the landlord that I'd have my after-dinner coffee in Brussels and be back in time for breakfast. I could have taken a walk in the countryside and come back spinning them any old yarn. Nobody would have cared. They just wanted to get through another night. But I took it further, promising to bring back the café receipt. It wasn't in the same league as the Paris-Dakar rally but it impressed the customers in Hazebrouck; some of them had never seen the sea, thirty miles away. If sea is the right word for what comes after the coast around Dunkirk. Bray les Dunes, Loon Beach, Wissant, Ambleteuse! There's a long way to go before these names have the same ring as Saint-Tropez, Ramateulle or Juan-les-Pins.

I had three hundred kilometres to do. The outward trip was fine. I reached Brussels by the Tournai road and found myself in the middle of a city disaster area, full of gaping holes, bristling with diversions and one-way systems. It took me nearly an hour to get to the old town, where a huge notice informed visitors how long the metro excavation work would last and thanking them for their forbearance. No shops were open and this absence of life reinforced my feeling of being in a city in wartime. I parked in the Grand' Place. A red light was shining under the arcades. I went up to the dimly lit window, dreaming by now of the mug of cold beer being set on the counter. I pushed open the door, ready to shout out my order to the barman. The astonishment of the officers on duty in the police station was just as great as mine.

That night I didn't just learn that a red light indicated the police station in the Grand' Place. I was also taught that a copper nail (I was even assured it was gold) set in the centre of the forecourt of Notre-Dame de Paris symbolised the starting point for the main French highways. That was in a bar on the outskirts, on the return journey, near Halle. I'd sat down on a high stool, next to what I thought at first sight was a pink flamingo. I had a look round as I drank the long-awaited beer. An outlying pick-up joint where my flamingo, a tart covered in pink muslin, was patiently waiting for any driver delayed on the road.

The owner, in a chatty mood, told me he'd lived in Paris before the war. He showed me some bottles of booze he boasted were his exclusive line. He couldn't say enough in praise of the kirsch cherry brandy; he made me drink a toast to Franco-Belgian friendship. Then he went on about the nail at Notre-Dame ...

The train reached Brussels Central just before half past eight. I took a taxi and asked for Jeu de Balle square.

— OK, it's just ahead but I have to go round by Saint Gudule, because of the roadworks.

— Still roadworks for the metro?

— Oh no, that's finished. Now it's the extension to the station. Look, there's Saint Gudule! Stuck between the Belgian National Bank and the Sabena Airlines building ... They're ruining everything in this country; just as if, where you come from, they'd decided to stick a shopping-mall on either side of the Notre-Dame towers? ... One of these days they'll put the Manneken-Pis in a public toilet and you'll have to put a coin in the slot to see it pee!

He dropped me at a corner of rue Haut and rue des

Renards. The square was blocked off with a police cordon; mention of Deril's name got me through. I headed straight for the director's van parked out of the way in rue Blaes. A man of around fifty, with greying hair skimming his shoulders, stared at me out of round, steel-rimmed spectacles.

— I have an appointment with M. Deril, the director.

— You've come to the right man, Inspector, that's me. Just give me a minute: I have to do some setting up for the overhead shots.

I watched him. In the midst of a group of technicians, he gave orders and listened to suggestions, nodding and shaking his head, waving his arms about, tossing his hair. He came back to the van, where I'd stayed.

— You spoke on the phone about a fleamarket. I was expecting to find the square full of tourists!

— That's for tomorrow morning, Inspector; we're filming it now as an empty expanse. The camera's going to track over the ground and across building frontages in a planned sequence. We'll follow exactly the same route when the market's in full swing tomorrow morning around eleven . . . Anyway, you haven't rushed here from Paris for a shoot about something you must be as familiar with as I am! The fleamarket wasn't invented in Brussels.

— No, and I don't have very much time.

— You aren't the first Frenchman to take an interest in this film of the Algerian demonstration. The security forces in your country tried to buy the original and the copies from Belgian TV, but our management refused. I suppose those responsible for the slaughter aren't keen on getting publicity for the outcome of their orders . . . Their request goes back twenty years. Just after an article containing a brief interview with Teerlock came out in *le Soir*. Until then I'm sure no one was aware that these reels of film existed.

— Except the controllers of your channel.

— Belgian television managed to free itself of political control long before its French counterparts ... There's no pressure put on journalists that would compel them to keep something under wraps. To be quite frank, we weren't in Paris to cover this demonstration, but to follow the Jacques Brel concerts at Olympia: I remember he was starting a fortnight's run the next day and they'd cancelled the rehearsal. Brel was bound by an old contract to attend a reception in the rooms of the naval ministry on the evening of 16 October. An amazing line-up: Jacques Brel, Charles Trenet, the orchestra of Jacques Hélian and ... Farah Dibah! We'd managed to get invitations for the reception at the Belgian embassy. Were you there during the official visit of the Shah of Iran and his wife?

— No, it's a pleasure that was denied me!

— Myself, I've rubbed shoulders with the crème de la crème. I don't know about Belgium, but seeing your Republican Guard turned out to honour the Emperor of Persia was beyond my comprehension. I've never understood what our Jacques was doing among that gang!

We had gone inside the production van. Deril sat down in front of a video monitor. He put in a cassette.

— I've checked, there's an hour and seven minutes for you. If there's anything you're particularly struck by, just make a note of the number on the counter and we can pull some stills for you. I'll leave you to it, I've still got work to do.

The images went by, in unbearable succession. The first half of the film had been shot from a car travelling from one part of Paris to another. Over and over again unarmed demonstrators were charged, terrified by compact groups of CRS and purposeful militia. The lack of sound gave even greater weight to the scenes of violence.

Suddenly the car stopped, taking up a discreet kerbside position. The cameraman's hand-held pan meant I could recognise the Porte de la Villette district. The old slaughterhouse buildings were still there and the Gravereau Bank building. The perspective ended with the black expanse of the Villette basin, where the Ourcq canal meets the Saint-Denis canal. The lens was suddenly tilted upwards and the cameraman used the zoom to pick out a group of men rushing up rue Corentin Cariou; they were heading towards the bridge. Their helmets and leather coats shone in the rain. Suddenly a body was thrown into the water. I could almost hear the splash as the corpse made contact with the water's surface. Another one followed, then another. The same movements repeated eleven times. Then back to the lights. The façade of the Rex, the poster for *The Guns of Navarone*. On a hoarding a black-and-white poster for the first Tornado vacuum-sweeper half-covered an advertising splash for a weekly part-work: starting on 25 October, THE WHOLE UNIVERSE, for one franc fifty a week.

A close-up plainly showed the face of a young Algerian woman, soon blanked out by a black uniform. When the policeman stood back, a man's face replaced the woman's; a truncheon came down. The camera angle changed again. A jukebox filled part of the image. It was probably the sequence Marc Rosner had told me about that very morning.

A detachment of militia circled a handful of demonstrators. City buses were parked further on, near rue du Sentier. The Algerians were bundled towards them. Packed, the buses left the stop one at a time. Bodies hung dangerously from the edge of the rear platform. The driver was alone with his human cargo. A hundred, a hundred and fifty prisoners. Yet none of them thought of escaping or freeing their comrades. Paris was caged in, all flight seemed doomed to failure.

The camera moved left up boulevard Bonne-Nouvelle. The cameraman focused on the window of the Madeleine Bastille café, then stopped at the corner of rue de Ville Neuve.

A CRS man was walking slowly along the pavement; he was taking off his coat, oblivious to the oddness of this action in the thick of a riot. He seemed unaware of the violence raging around him, just as he seemed unaware of the rain. The cameraman didn't linger on this strange scene; he pulled back a few metres to settle on the body of someone who had been injured. Thirty seconds passed, interminably, before the camera moved forward again. The CRS man was walking on, still unhurried. He passed rue Thorel. When he got to rue Notre-Dame de Bonne-Nouvelle, he stopped short, as if hesitating, then turned off and climbed the steps. There was another man there; he was carrying a bouquet of flowers and a package of cakes. The CRS man moved beside him.

In the foreground Algerians were being rounded up, hands behind their heads. A captain was making a determined effort to restrain his men, who were in a frenzy and wouldn't stop hitting the prisoners. The next shots were outside the Paris Opéra, which the police were cordoning off for the protection of the audience at Rameau's *Les Indes Galantes.* Then the screen went blank. I pressed the stop button and waited for Deril to come back. Through the window I saw him checking the direction of the floodlights, altering the path of the beams. When he finished this work he came to get me in the van.

— Well, any surprises, Inspector? You're looking pleased . . .

I nodded.

— Yes, I recognised the fellow I was looking for. The

image is around 813, near the end of the tape. If you turn this machine on again, I can show you.

He viewed the sequence, took out the cassette and asked one of his assistants to go to the studios and make a print of the scene where the CRS man is by the railings, at the steps next to Roger Thiraud. He gripped me by the shoulder.

— Come and have dinner with me, Inspector. You can't leave Brussels without paying your respects to our cuisine. They'll still be setting up here for another two hours. It's crazy the time we waste hanging around! But the movies are like that. You have a team of fifty people, working one after the other, each of them doing a terrific job in a way that no one else would do it. But in the end it's the director who goes off for dinner and pockets all the compliments when he gets back! Come on, I'll take you to My Father Mustache. There's nothing like it in France. It's an old cinema that went out of business and was bought up by a student organisation. They replaced the cinema seats with rows of wooden benches and tables. They serve Belgian specialities. Every fifteen minutes they turn out the lights and show silent shorts: Laurel and Hardy, Harold Lloyd, Charlie Chaplin or Buster Keaton. Two or three times a night they let a singer or a band have a go. They're usually buskers. English, German, Japanese, all different nationalities get a look in.

He recommended a dish from Namur, *l'anguille à l'escavèche*; he ordered two large mugs of Krieks.

— You'll see, it's first rate, saltwater eel pickled then roasted. They serve it cold, in aspic. By the way, do you know that the same river flows through our two capitals?

— No, you're wrong there, the Seine has its source near Dijon; it flows into the Channel between le Havre and Honfleur, and never leaves France.

He roared with laughter.

— Oh, you French are always so touchy about your country! Of course the Seine doesn't flow past the respectable façades of Place de Broukere, but almost ... Our river is called the Senne, with two n's. You've got off lightly! Brussels is a city worthy of Alphonse Allais: go along the boulevards of the Petite Ceinture which follow the old fortifications. The boulevard de Waterloo isn't very far from the boulevard de l'Abattoir.

After the eel, we went back to Jeu de Balle square where the still I'd wanted from the footage was waiting for me. Deril called a taxi and insisted on paying the fare. I promised to keep him informed about the progress of my investigation.

The beer had its after-effects in the train heading back to Paris. I understood why this good-natured nation had chosen the Manneken-Pis as its emblem.

CHAPTER SIX

Madame Thiraud agreed to see me late the following afternoon. I used the time I had until this meeting to stroll around the city. I reached the boulevards ahead of time and, almost without thinking, I retraced the steps of the CRS man twenty years earlier, as filmed by the Belgian crew. Little had changed since then, apart from the poster at the Rex, now advertising a Walt Disney cartoon, and the cafeteria at *l'Humanité*, which had become a Burger King.

I crossed the boulevard opposite the Madeleine-Bastille, whose tables took up most of the pavement. A group of Japanese tourists all in white shirts and blouses were getting off a doubledecker Paris-Vision bus, and pointing at the Gymnase Theatre whose frontage announced Guy Bedos's new show. I was even more suprised when they all followed the guide right into the foyer. I went up in the direction of Porte Saint-Denis, passing rue de la Ville Neuve and rue Thorel. Rue Notre-Dame de Bonne-Nouvelle sloped upwards and didn't run straight on to the boulevard. On this side it ended at two flights of steps; one wide and slightly curved, the other narrow and straight. Once you'd climbed one or other of these stairways, you entered a district that was altogether different from the boulevards. The flashy shop signs and neon-lit cafés gave

way to the busy muddle of the rag trade. From rue
Beauregard onwards the sewing machine reigned, a
hardworking world of dressmakers and cutters, seam-
stresses and embroiderers who often had the tall,
sturdy looks of new arrivals from the Anatolian plain or
the Nile valley, or else tiny Asian refugees from Indo-
China. Pakistani or Bengali storekeepers, their turbaned
heads a flash of whiteness, wheeled along gigantic rolls
of cloth, their carts dodging dogs, cars and passers-by,
as they moved between the pavement and the roadway.

Tucked between the boulevards and rue Beauregard,
rue Notre-Dame de Bonne-Nouvelle was an island of
calm; the towering presence of the church that gave it
its name had a lot to do with this. I took my place at the
bar of the Fifteen Steps and ordered a beer that was
served to me by a waiter who had only one hand. For
the next few minutes I didn't take my eyes off him; I was
amazed by his dexerity at squeezing lemons, making
hot dogs, spreading sandwiches with paté, while he
balanced glasses, bread or salami with his stump. The
owner came and leant in front of me. He looked quickly
over at the barman and back to me.

— You can't believe it, eh! Your first time here?

I told him it was.

— It makes an impression on the customers, but like
everything else you get used to it.

He jerked his chin in the barman's direction.

— He's an old armaments worker, like me. We
worked together in explosives, nitroglycerine. I got out
in one piece! He wasn't so lucky. I threw my hand in and
he left his behind . . . You have to see the funny side.

— How did it happen? An accident?

— Yes, but to begin with no one knew why. He'd been
working with nitroglycol day in day out for years, like
me, without a hitch. Then one day, when he'd just
started work after the holidays, he goes and drops a

flask. Instead of taking cover and protecting himself, he tried to catch it. You see the result . . .

— Yes, the hazards of the job.

— Yes, Monsieur, that's what everybody said. But the guys doing scientific research noticed from their statistics that this kind of accident happened most often on Mondays or after holidays. When they looked into it a bit more they realised that nitroglycol had an effect on the heart. A bit like a drug! When you were working you really did feel well. On weekends and holidays it was quite the opposite: we were deprived of the nitro fumes. Since then they've developed a nitroglycerine-based medication for people with heart complaints; it dilates the coronaries . . .

— In other words your barman wasn't the victim of an industrial accident, his hand came off as the result of an occupational disease!

— I never saw it that way . . .

I paid for my beer and left the Fifteen Steps. On the locksmith's booth that backed on to the side of the stairs, a notice promised keys made while you wait, while a hand-written note stuck on the glass announced: Back in 15 minutes.

Number five rue Notre-Dame de Bonne-Nouvelle turned out to be an old Paris building in good repair, with fretwork blinds at the windows. On the wall to the left of the street door a white marble plaque announced in gold letters: National Union of Crane Operators. I crossed a tiny garden to get to the door. I was now in the entrance hall which was embellished with an absurd neo-Greek relief whose figures played a flute and pan pipes. Pinned to the glass of the caretaker's door was a list of tenants with their floor and apartment number. The waxed steps of the wooden staircase squeaked as I trod on them. The first floor was adorned with a wide gilt-edged mirror and a rustic painting in shades of brown. I reached the third a little out of breath and knocked hard several times before Madame Thiraud answered. Three locks were undone in succession, then the door opened a few centimetres, with the safety chain on.

— Madame, I am Inspector Cadin, I spoke to you this morning.

The door slammed shut again while the chain was undone. At last I made my way into the apartment.

Roger Thiraud's widow couldn't have been more than forty-five, but her self-imposed seclusion had turned her into an old woman. She preceded me along the corridor, stooping, with knees bent and feet dragging. She seemed to slide along the floor noiselessly. The smallest movement appeared to require a painful effort. With a heavy sigh she sank into an armchair with a crocheted woollen cover. She stared at me vacantly.

The room was in darkness. All the shutters had been closed; she had left one window open just enough to let some air in. A few rays of sunlight filtered through the latticework. I pulled a chair up to the table and sat down.

— As I told you this morning, I'm investigating your son Bernard's death. So far this murder is a total mystery; we have very little to go on. We know of no enemies, his love life seemed quite straightforward ... To be quite honest, though, there's an event that does interest me, before your son's time: his father's death ...

I watched her reactions, but there was no response at the mention of her husband's death.

— In the course of my inquiry I've learned something of the circumstances in which your husband died. I've got no proof at all, but it is possible that your son was murdered for the same reasons as his father. Don't you think?

I might as well have been talking to a brick wall, a

corpse. Madame Thiraud kept her eyes trained on me, but never quite focusing, as if she was looking past me far into the distance. I went on.

— I also know that there was no inquiry in 1961 and that your husband featured as an official victim of the Algerian demonstration. Whose victim? There's room for doubt. It isn't too late to remedy this. I want to do my bit.

For the first time she stirred; she got up and came towards me, leaning on a dresser for support.

— Inspector, this is all in the past. It's futile to go back over everything that happened and start analysing who's to blame . . .

Every word was followed by a long pause and she punctuated her speech with deep breaths.

— My husband is dead, my son is dead. You won't bring them back. I am resigned; I hope to join them as soon as possible.

— Why, what do you have to hide? Roger Thiraud was shot while taking part in a demonstration. Did you know that he was involved in an FLN aid network?

— You're wrong. My husband had no inclination for politics. He was interested in his work, in history. His time was entirely taken up with it, at school and at home. On the evening of his death he was coming home after his last lesson, as usual . . .

She moved about the room like an old woman, carefully avoiding the area near the windows that overlooked the street. Curious, I went over to them, but this drove her into a real panic. She pressed herself back against the facing wall, panting. The surface surrounding the window was a kind of no man's land covered in layers of dust. No one ever came near this spot. With one quick movement I caught hold of the curtains and pulled them back. The bolt was stiff. It took a bit of effort to get the window open. I raised the latch on the shutters. Daylight invaded the apartment; a shaft of sunlight shone across the wall where Madame Thiraud stood. I leaned out. Ten metres down people were bustling past the locksmith's booth whose curved roof was all that was visible. A group of young boys were climbing the steps of rue Notre-Dame de Bonne-Nouvelle.

Madame Thiraud had fled to the kitchen, in a fit of hysterics. She was in tears, her body shuddering and twitching. I put my arm round her.

— I wish you no harm, Madame. I'm here to help you. Don't be afraid . . .

I held her by the wrists and pulled her gently towards the dreaded spot, talking to her and comforting her with every step. The closer she got to the window the more intense her distress became. She protested but let herself be led, giving up all resistance. I stood her next to me with her arms supported by the sill.

— Open your eyes, I beg you. It's twenty-one years now, you have no more to fear.

She relaxed and her crying and whimpering stopped. Her eyes flickered open, barely at all at first, then closed again. The lashes moved again. She made up her mind all at once to look at the street.

— You were here, weren't you? You were waiting for him when he was killed? Tell me . . . Did no one ever ask you to give evidence?

She moved quietly away from the window and sat in the armchair again. The ordeal had changed her; she seemed stronger, younger, as if returned to her real age. She turned towards me.

— Yes, I was by the window. Roger finished his last lesson at five. He should have been back a good two hours earlier. It was a period when I was very anxious. I was pregnant with Bernard, a very difficult pregnancy that kept me from going out. I'd been told I had to stay at home or I'd risk a premature birth. Roger hadn't told me he'd be late. And then, out of the blue, the demonstration started. Shouting, pushing, explosions of teargas, gunshot. I was crazy with worry. I kept rushing to the window to look for my husband, or to the door the moment I heard steps on the stairs. Then I saw him in the street, making his way home. I remember it as if I were seeing it all over again. He was walking along with a bouquet of mimosa and a box of cakes. He climbed some of the steps then stopped to look down at what was happening, the truncheon beatings. I shouted to him to come up, not to linger, but my voice couldn't be heard above the noise of the demonstration.

— Was he alone?

— He was at first, but then a man in a police uniform, a CRS I think, came up next to him. There was something odd about him, he had his leather coat folded over his arm, even though it was cold and wet. Then he slipped behind my husband, catching his head in an armlock. He had a revolver in his other hand. I shouted, shouted out as loud as I could, but it made no difference. I wanted to go down there but I could hardly cross this room, because of Bernard ... I mean because of my belly. Poor Bernard!

— Forgive me for making you stir up such terrible memories, but there was no other way. A Belgian filmmaker shot part of this scene. He was on the other side of the boulevard, near the Gymnase Theatre. I have a still photograph taken from his film. It shows your husband just before he died. His murderer's face is half-concealed but it gives us plenty to go on. Will you take a look at it?

She agreed to. I took out the print made the night before in Brussels.

— Do you recognise him?

She shook her head.

— No, Inspector, I've never met this man. I never saw my husband with any policeman and I don't understand why they killed him . . .

— One last thing, Madame, and I'll have finished. You told me a moment ago that your husband finished teaching at five o'clock. How do you account for him only getting here some two hours later? It's less than a ten-minute walk from the lycée to the boulevard . . .

— I have no explanation.

— Was he often late?

— Once a week, sometimes twice . . . Listen, Inspector, my pregnancy ruled out any physical intimacy. It's a hard thing to have to say but it's the truth. I acknowledge that Roger needed to be with another woman. What's wrong with that?

— Nothing. I'm sorry, but there's no place for discretion in my job. I asked you this question because the inventory of what they found in Roger Thiraud's pockets mentions a cinema ticket. From the Midi-Minuit to be precise. I think we have the answer there! Twenty years ago a respectable history teacher would have been reluctant to confess his taste for horror films. Even to his wife. I have the ticket number: I'll get one of my subordinates to check the date it was issued with the National Cinema Centre.

She gave me a smile; it hurt me to realize that this was her first smile for twenty-two years.

— Your husband wasn't killed by accident. It's clear that his murderer was following a definite plan, that he knew exactly who he was looking for. The Belgian film makes this clear. The CRS man, or let's say the man in CRS guise, came into the open and made straight for rue Notre-Dame de Bonne-Nouvelle. His methods demonstrate that we're dealing with a professional, as with your son's murder in Toulouse. Or, which is unlikely, your husband was another target's double.

No, I think he was the killer's intended target. Your husband was in someone's way, so much so that he became the victim of an execution. Are you sure that he wasn't involved in politics, or any trade union or even human rights activities?

— No, I've already told you. Apart from that lateness, those outings to the cinema, if I'm to take your word for it, I see no mysteries in my husband's life. Roger never brought these things up at home. He talked about history or literature. He was passionately interested in the Middle Ages and in his spare time he was writing a kind of monograph on Drancy, where he was born. He was really fond of his parents — they still live there in rue du Bois-de-l'Amour. I still think it might have been that house that got him interested in history . . .

— What do you mean?

— To begin with the building was part of a farm that became a restaurant at the turn of the century. For a few years it was known mostly as a house of ill repute. After the Marthe Richard Law against brothels was passed, it was three-quarters demolished to build a maternity clinic. My husband was born there. He spent his entire childhood just round the corner, in a house that had survived the renovation of that quarter. This can't be of much interest to you, I realise. To get to the point, this monograph is with my son. That's to say with his fiancée, Claudine. Do you know her?

— Yes, I met her in Toulouse. I'd like to take a look at that piece of work. I was planning to talk with her before leaving tomorrow evening. Did they get along well?

— To be honest I have no idea. It was difficult for her coming here: Bernard always had to persuade her. I knew she was ill at ease in my company, but I just wasn't up to it. I'm not easy to be with. They seemed as if they were happy together, that's all I can remember.

•

I left her then and made my way down the waxed stairs gingerly, keeping my hand on the banister. I turned left towards the boulevards. When I got halfway down the steps of rue Notre-Dame de Bonne-Nouvelle, I turned and looked up towards Madame Thiraud's apartment. She was leaning at the windowsill. She gave me a friendly wave. I watched her for a moment before returning her greeting, then I went down into the metro. At Auber I transferred on to the suburban line. Dalbois had told me to go as far as the last stop at Marne la Vallée.

A pedestrian passage, under domed plexi glass, led from the station to the forecourt where the town's bus routes converged. One glance was enough to show me that this was the sum total of local transport!

The square was set at the centre of a valley with overhanging hills. Its western side was bounded by a huge shopping mall. The only fancy touch was a pink building, some twenty storeys high, perched on top of one of the hills. In fact the bus I was sitting in went right past this building so I was able to get a good look at it. The outside was a fair imitation of the façade of a Spanish bullring, a kind of long circular wall honeycombed with cavities. Every twenty metres a semicircular column hugged the whole height of the building. Openings cut into these towers revealed lift cabins. A wide arcade showed off a vast courtyard planted with trees and flowers. A business sign listed the names and addresses of the contractors with the information: 'The Arena. Six hundred and thirty luxury apartments overlooking the Marne. One and two bedrooms. Loans available.'

The driver called out the stop for Pyramid. Dalbois had told me to go past an office block, then turn left towards the water tower. He was living on a housing estate, halfway between apartments and individual houses. The dwelling 'modules' took the form of cubes stacked together in what seemed to be no particular order. The roof of the lower section was also the terrace of the upper one. I rang the bell of 73. Dalbois opened the door.

— Good evening, Cadin, I was wondering whether you were going to show up.

I started back in surprise to make the point that the idea hadn't even occurred to me.

— Listen, I'm very happy to accept your invitation.

I was introduced to Giselle, who was busy preparing dinner. She closed the electronic oven and turned to me, pointing at her apron.

— I'm sorry, but I haven't had time to change yet.

Dalbois showed me round every nook and cranny of his apartment, then took me into the sitting room. He switched on the television, carefully turning down the sound.

— Well, making progress?

I told him about my Brussels trip and my interview with Bernard Thiraud's mother. He got interested when I mentioned the print the Belgian television technicians had made from the video tape.

— Have you got this picture on you?

I put it down on the low table among the aperitif tidbits and bottles of spirits.

— Your story is just amazing . . .

He peered at the print.

— Your CRS guy looks genuine enough. Apart from having no insignia. By rights he should have been wearing his company and district numbers. Don't you think?

— Under normal circumstances, yes. But not that night. I found out that regulations were suspended. All units were using reserve weapons, including firearms. It would make sense that the men had been given orders to cover their identification codes.

— You've got mixed up in a strange old business. I've already given you this advice but I don't mind repeating it. Drop it. Dig around in Toulouse to your heart's content. Nobody expects any more from you. It'll end with a file classified Case Closed. What have you got to lose? Nothing! You'll easily find yourself another murder case that stinks less. A pastis?

— No thanks? I can't drink in this heat.

— Well, let's eat. I chose the menu, in memory of our years of hard labour in Strasbourg.

Giselle Dalbois simpered in with a terracotta dish piled high with *choucroute au boudin blanc*, and set it between two bottles of Gewürztraminer.

— Tuck in, Cadin, don't be shy. You'll see she's pretty good. It's a Strasbourg choucroute for special occasions. Giselle cooks it the way they do in Colmar: she adds a glass of kirsch an hour before serving it. What do you think?

— Excellent. My congratulations, Madame.

We'd finished the lot, generously helped by the Alsace wine. Giselle served our coffee on the terrace, where it was cool. Dalbois leaned towards me, wearing a serious expression, as if to impart a confidence.

— You know, Cadin, we're a minority . . .

Then he dropped his conspiratorial air.

— In the morning eight out of ten French people drink coffee. Only four of them indulge at lunchtime. Only two in the afternoon and only one after dinner! Well, we three are that one!

He looked at his watch, feigning surprise.

— You'll have to hurry, your last train leaves in twenty minutes. I'd have asked you to stay the night, but the kids' beds are on the short side.

I made sure not to insist . . . Family life, even other people's, doesn't suit me. They took me to the station. On the way I gave the film still to Dalbois.

— Do me one last favour; try to get something on this guy. It won't be easy to track him down, especially since he's bound to have been retired by now. If you don't come up with anything I'll think about your advice.

He tucked the picture in the inside pocket of his jacket. The train came in. I took a seat by the window and rolled it down, despite all the *pericoloso sporgersi* warnings. On the platform Dalbois was on tiptoe so as to keep his voice down.

— I'm promising nothing, Cadin. Give me three or four days. If I'm going to come up with something that's all I'll need. No messing, your CRS guy is more dangerous than a stick of dynamite; all I want is to get shot of his ugly mug as quickly as I can. I'll call you in Toulouse when I've got some news. Ciao.

The compartment was empty. I was alone as far as Vincennes. Then a gang of louts took over. A big pimply guy came over to me. He sat down heavily on the seat opposite and stretched his legs across with his shoes less than a centimetre from my thigh. My response was to push back the right flap of my jacket to display the black butt of my revolver and its holster. Immediately the two feet came into contact with the floor. The fellow got up, rather nervously. I heard a few snatches of conversation: It's a cop, he's got a gun. They decided to get off at the next station, Nation, and I was left in peace again.

•

It didn't knock me out. No . . . but a little flutter of the heart all the same, when I recognised Claudine Chenet's voice on the phone the next morning. I'd been keen to see her though I'd been in two minds. I'd think up one opening gambit, then change it . . . Her call put an end to all this dithering.

— Inspector, I just want to thank you. Bernard's mother got in touch with me last night to tell me how things had gone with you. I don't know if this meeting was of any use to your enquiry, I hope so, but the very fact that you are trying to find out why Bernard was killed makes a difference to us.

I could only mumble pitiably, so I let her take over again.

— Are you going back to Toulouse tonight? Is that right?

I thought I detected a trace of displeasure, almost regret, in the way she spoke.

— Yes, I'm taking the four o'clock train. Could we see one another before then? I won't go into it, but I still have some questions to ask you. What are you doing for lunch?

— I'm working on my thesis.

— And I thought students were always on holiday!

My remark was rather thoughtless. Her reply had no anger in it.

— In that case they're very sad holidays . . . I'm happier working, it takes my mind off things. Anyway, what I'm working on is pleasant enough. But lunch time would be fine. I'm doing some field work, between Porte d'Italie and Porte de Gentilly. There's a little café on boulevard Kellerman, just after the entrance to the Charlety stadium. We could meet there around one. It's called the Stadium.

I okayed the time and place, then hung up. I spent a few minutes packing, then went down to the hotel lounge where two guests with nothing better to do were watching the TV news on Channel One. Yann Morousi was announcing the death in tragic circumstances of one of the founding fathers of video. His fulsome panegyric ended with the announcement:

— So on the occasion of the death of this illustrious precursor of our profession, we are happy to present this interview of less than a week ago ...

The studio technicians must have signalled to him that this happiness was inappropriate to the nature of the event, for Marousi's face changed. He went on.

— Here then is the interview that our editors have the sad privilege of dedicating to the memory of this pioneer of new techniques.

I could stand no more. I paid my bill, carefully pocketed the receipt, for expenses, and made for the nearest metro station. I got off at Maison Blanche, which meant I came out on boulevard Kellerman by the Republican Guard barracks.

Claudine was waiting for me at the back of the café. The bar was besieged by rugby supporters who were celebrating in advance their team's victory in the afternoon match.

I'd had a substantial breakfast so a glass of mineral water was all I wanted.

— Well, I'm ready for your questions, Inspector.

She had spoken in a voice filled with emotion, as if somehow this conversation had become important to her. As far as I was concerned, nothing had changed since our silent journey, with me left high and dry at a taxi rank. Things were going too fast for my liking, even though it was the right direction!

I immediately assumed an expression of professional blandness.

— Do I seem so insensitive? There are only a few details I want to know. We have no new information that could explain your fiancé's execution. Nothing, unless what happened to his father. Which makes it all the more complicated ...

She interrupted:

— But you have a lead, my mother-in-law told me about the photograph ...

— Yes, I'm hoping to get to this CRS guy. He's certainly the one who shot Roger Thiraud in 1961. I'm not counting on it; the odds of tracking him down are one in a hundred. The only hypothesis worth considering is a link between the two murders. Yet that doesn't fit with what happened in Toulouse. Why would the murderer have taken so many risks?

I took Claudine's hand when she put it on the table to lift her cup. Rather than withdrawing it she turned her palm against mine and our fingers touched. I forced myself to speak, but it was no longer questions and answers we needed. These had to give way to a new way of talking.

— Have you thought of all this since you came back? Try. . . . Did Bernard ever mention the events of the Algerian war, especially towards the end?

— No, I've already told you so. Bernard never told me about his problems. We talked mostly about our studies, what we planned to do later. When it came to other things we got by ... which wasn't easy ... his mother, as you've seen, was in a terrible state. She practically never set foot outside. Fortunately, he kept closely in touch with his grandparents. It was a relief to spend the day with them. They live in the suburbs, an old house at Drancy ... it's Seine-Saint-Denis, but you'd think you were hundreds of kilometres from Paris, in the real countryside. They have a garden with an orchard. From what I could see Bernard's mother was very shocked by her husband's death, so much that she refused to bring up her son. It was the grandparents who took care of him. . . . You ought to meet them, they're very warm, welcoming people. At the same time they thought their son had been given back to them, thirty years later; they planned Bernard's upbringing as if he was their own child. They never attempted to resume contact with their daughter-in-law, from fear of being separated from Bernard. I can understand them . . . In a way.

She was talking very fast, her head lowered so as to avoid my eyes. She was trying to explain things without reopening too many wounds. Suddenly she was on her feet and lighthearted again.

— This time I'm buying the drinks, I'm in your debt. Don't act surprised. I remember you tipping the hotel porter. I haven't paid you back yet!

Outside she took my arm and guided me through the housing projects on rue Thomire and avenue Caffieri. We reached Poterne des Peupliers in silence. Under the stone bridge of the circle railway, a pack of dogs were vying in their attacks on a rubbish skip left there by the municipality to relieve Parisians of their vast quantities of rubbish. A yellow-haired alsatian had won: he was standing at the top of the heap. As we approached he showed two rows of threatening teeth, obliging us to cross to the opposite pavement.

Claudine turned into rue Max Jacob, which climbs in a gentle slope towards the Italie quarter. You could make out glass and steel towers behind the red-brick buildings. In the middle of a bend in the road she turned right towards a green-painted metal gate and pushed it open. In front of me was a vast public garden planted with trees, its different levels linked by imposing stone steps. Claudine pointed out the loopholed ramparts.

— We are on the remains of the fortifications of Paris! There's not a lot left, they've been knocking it down since 1920. The last bastions were demolished when they were building the ring road. I found this intact stretch during a walk. In the middle of the Porte de Charenton exit there's a corner battlement that's been turned into an office of works. . . . It was Thiers who had them built, starting in 1842 . . . thirty kilometres of defence works. The irony is that he led the attack on them during the Paris Commune in 1871!

We had reached the edge of the ramparts. We were looking down on a vast open space which contained a children's playground laid out with games, rope frames, slides. To the right the garden abutted the seething mass of the ring road and to the left the housing projects. Further, on the horizon, a multitude of small buildings announced the start of the suburbs: Arcueil, Kremlin-Bicêtre. On the flank of the hill, tucked between the motorway and the big projects, was Gentilly cemetery. Claudine took in the whole scene with a sweep of her arm.

— See how calm it is. Yet after the battlements were built thousands of people settled here.

— Did they have the right to do that?

— No. By rights it was prohibited, but sometimes laws yield to realities; the housing shortage and high rents for example. Like squatters today . . . It's not so long ago that it was our grandparents who lived in shanty towns! This was one of the most sordid districts, like the area round Porte Saint-Ouen. The kingdom of the rag pickers. No water, gas or electricity. All the sewage went straight into a stream that flowed through a hollow at the bottom of the cemetery. The Bièvre, a real open sewer . . . I'm boring you?

— Not at all. I was only thinking that you didn't stand much chance of a job with the city of Paris tourist office! Go on. Listening to you I get the impression that you're nostalgic for those days. I'm not; this neck of the woods must have been a den of crooks and murderers. A court of miracles.

— Of course, it was like that. But that's only one aspect of it. It was also like scenes from *Casque d'Or* and the settings of Le Breton's books . . . On Sundays, the slopes of the ramparts looked like the Senlis woods, with families on an outing. There were even ponds and people fished . . .

— Plenty of cafés too!

— Bound to be! You see, I'm more nostalgic for pleasure gardens than vans selling hot dogs! Of course there were brawls, settling of scores, but dance halls are seldom trouble free, are they? People came to forget the tiredness of a week's work. In those days people did sixty hours' hard graft in dreadful conditions. Legend and literature have neglected this side of things. It was easier to talk about the barbarians at the city gates.

— Believe me, criminals can't have had much trouble finding a hideway in that undergrowth of shanties!

— Maybe, but a few decades earlier, every crime under the sun was put down to the working-class districts. Take a newspaper, open it at the *faits divers*, and you'll find that nothing much has changed. The black sheep are now the ones living in the big housing projects in the outer suburbs. The Minguette flats, the 4000. The immigrants have replaced the vagrants, the young unemployed have succeeded the rag pickers.

— You won't convince me that the criminals weren't thick on the ground! There are figures . . .

— No, they did exist, in fact in the same proportion as for Paris and the Seine département. Neither more nor less. There were those with an interest in giving a negative image to the poorer sections of the working class. They made use of this outcast status to push them beyond the city limits. This continues today in the way everyday insecurities are played on. There's an attempt to identify the social groups most hard hit by the crisis as groups endangering the rest of society. A real sleight of hand! Victims are turned into bogeymen. And it

works! The kindliest old lady will hug her bag to her
chest the minute she encounters a boy whose complexion is on the dark side. Only this kind of fear can
legitimise the measures that are then taken against
these people.

— You're forgetting you're talking to a cop . . .

She smiled and pressed her arm more tightly against
mine.

— No, not for a minute. Go and look at the police
registers in the days of the fortifications. The work of
your ancestors, as it were! Bloodshed was extremely
rare. The most common crimes were petty swindles,
the theft of food, family brawls. Yet the great majority
of headlines in the gutter press ooze with blood. Good
for selling newsprint! Popular newspapers today have
not changed: murderers, sadists, rapists, all the filthy
roles are played by workers, have-nots. Never any big
shots . . . Doctors, lawyers, captains of industry get
mentioned on the Society page. They get off lightly,
when in fact the sums involved in fraud and embezzle-
ment cases add up to ten times the total of all hold-ups
throughout France.

— So what you're saying is you think we're chasing
the wrong villains?

— You only chase the little ones and you let the big
ones prosper undisturbed . . .

— You don't know me, my earlier cases prove the
contrary . . .

I wanted to say more, so that she wouldn't see me as a
bastard timeserving cop, though without seeming to
justify myself. I tried out some words in my head but
the dialectic left me in the lurch. I took refuge in silence.
Claudine noticed my hestitation; she made the most of
it to launch another onslaught.

— The system has a good line in self-protection. The
police play a crucial role. Now and then an expiatory

victim has to be found to show that the upper echelons can be contaminated. And to prove that their strength lies in the fact that they can get rid of the bad elements without compunction. Landru, Petiot. . . They get everything thrown at them and are made into monsters whose function is to show how aberrant their behaviour is: everything places it outside the norm. On the other hand, the unemployed man who robs a grocery is seen as part of everyday life. He is taken as representing his class and surroundings. He becomes merely a product of his environment and not of a system that condemns him to poverty and theft.

— By your logic all the unemployed would be villains! Fortunately that's not the case.

She gave a heavy sigh. As her breast swelled it lifted the front of her summer blouse. I glimpsed the black lace flash of her bra. My heart abandoned its steady beat and started racing.

— You're not listening. I'll admit that there's one kind of equality between a company director and a down and out; there's the same odds of either becoming a sex maniac! However, you won't convince me that the unemployed man doesn't have more opportunity to be tempted by petty theft for simple reasons of survival.

Claudine was getting carried away. Her intensity coloured her cheeks the same red that her half-glimpsed breast had lit in mine. I surrendered.

— We won't agree on this . . . We already have some common ground, we mustn't forget that; I'll do my very best to arrest Bernard's murderer. Whether he's weak or strong, tramp or millionaire. Before I forget, Madame Thiraud mentioned something to me, a pamphlet, a monograph on Drancy that her husband was writing in his spare time. Do you know anything about it?

Claudine nodded.

— Yes, it's at home. Bernard wanted to finish it in

memory of his father. I can send it to you in Toulouse
tomorrow if you think it's relevant to the inquiry.

— It's better if I see it right away. I could drop in at
your place on my way to to the station. I'll ask the taxi to
make a detour . . .

She wrote her address in a notebook, tore out the
page and gave it to me.

Seven hours later, I arrived at Toulouse Central.
Sergeant Lardenne was waiting for me on the platform,
even though he'd been off duty since late afternoon. He
dropped me at my place, using the journey to bring me
up to date on the video games front. He'd even
managed to beat his son at the Battle of the Malvinas.
Four Exocets against two! A great score . . . By the sound
of it nothing more noteworthy had happened in my
absence.

CHAPTER SEVEN

Well, Bourrassol, anything on those bogus summonses?

The staff sergeant was sitting in my office. By the look of it he hadn't got very far.

He started spluttering.

— No, I mean, maybe ... Prodis's office at the Capitole seems to have something.

The name made me jump.

— Let's be clear, Bourrassol: I won't be in debt to Prodis. You well know that you have to repay guys like him a hundred times over! They think they're God almighty. You're the one who's responsible for flushing out these jokers. Nobody else. We were the only targets in this business, not the town hall. It's an internal problem as far as I'm concerned. And what's their story?

Bourrassol cleared his throat before answering.

— During the cantonal elections in '81, a newspaper poster, I mean a fake, was plastered all over town. It showed the official candidate practically naked on a beach in the arms of a young woman. Three months before that he'd had a car crash; he was basing part of his campaign on the theme of fear ... Holding meetings on crutches, you get the picture! The headline of the fake poster played on it: 'His car accident? The revenge of a jealous husband!' He filed a complaint against persons unknown, with the usual lack of results. Last week while they were working on an extension to the municipal print shop, the builders came across the offset plates that had been used for the poster. The staff were questioned. One of them confessed that he'd been in a situationist group active in Toulouse since 1976.

— Did he talk about the summonses for the anti-terrorist dossier?

— No, he admitted involvement between '77 and '82. He claimed the collective had then broken up, as the result of ideological differences. It's possible that some members of the group kept up their subversive activities, but in more difficult circumstances, given they no longer had the resources. Their forte was printing pamphlets and posters and reproducing official documents. Without the support of the guy from the municipal print shop they had to fall back on a straight printer . . .

— In which case it won't be too hard to corner them. Did they find out who were the other members of the network?

Bourrassol had been fiddling with a sheet of paper since the start of the interview; he put it down on the edge of the desk. I took the typed sheet and read out the names.

— Jacques Maunoury, Claude Anchel, Jean-Pierre Bourrassol . . .

I stopped short on this last name and questioned the sergeant.

— Is he related to you?

He bowed his head like a thieving urchin caught red-handed, and made a barely audible reply.

— Yes, Inspector, it's my son. I've done my letter of resignation. I've no idea what made him do it.

He sank back into his chair and broke down sobbing. I had no idea how to deal with this situation; I was out of my depth. I went over to Bourrassol and patted him on the shoulder as I'd seen people do in films.

— It's not that bad, Sergeant. What you've just done took a lot of courage. I can appreciate what it means to you. There can't be many policemen of your calibre who are ready to sacrifice their family to their ideal of justice and truth. You didn't shrink from turning in your own son! What more can be asked of a police officer? It would be adding to injustice to make you resign over something you didn't do. All said and done, they didn't do much harm. I'll try and sort it out.

Bourrassol had stopped weeping; he sniffled loudly before wiping his nose with the sleeve of his uniform.

— Have you discussed all this with your son? It was pretty easy for him to get hold of our headed paper and the rubber stamps. No one would have suspected the son of a colleague . . .

He answered me in a broken voice.

— Of course, I've thought of that too, but it's impossible, my son's been in the West Indies for four months. He's a conscript in the navy. I can't vouch for anything else . . . But as far as this is concerned he's got a watertight alibi.

The telephone cut short the sorry story of the Bourrassol family. It informed me of a hold-up taking place at a jeweller's in allée Jean-Jaurès. The salesman had managed to activate the alarm signal without being noticed. If we moved fast, we had a chance of catching the thieves red-handed. I checked my Heckler pistol, a PS9 model, and released the safety catch. Lardenne was waiting for me in the courtyard, the engine running. I got in next to him. He was getting a blow by blow account of the robbery on FM. He didn't need to be told to step on it.

A patrol car was out of sight behind the church of Notre-Dame des Graces. I radioed instructions to make no move until Lardenne gave the order. They were covering the jeweller's shop-front and the two streets either side of it. Going round the other way, we came down one of these streets. I got the car to stop just before the corner of allée Jean-Jaurès. I left Lardenne and sauntered towards the shop, trying to look like a casual passer-by. It didn't come easy; at moments like this you wish cop training contained one or two courses in body language ... I had a quick look around. I could see no one keeping lookout on the pavement. Unless they had an accomplice hiding in a doorway. Which would mean I was a perfect target.

When I got to the jeweller's I hurled myself against the glass door. I burst into the shop yelling like crazy, my gun drawn.

— Police! Drop your weapons.

The crook, an edgy little guy dressed like a bank clerk – Woolmark and Italian shoes – did a half turn on his heels and aimed a high-calibre weapon at my chest. He was at least as scared as I was.

— Don't get any ideas ... I'd have three bullets in your head before you'd got as far as pressing the trigger.

My thumb moved a fraction against the side of the pistol; it pressed gently on the tiny lever to the left behind the trigger. The slightest pressure on the trigger, the smallest movement of my index finger, would now release it.

— Listen carefully. When it comes to a situation like this my word is as good as gold. Better than anything you'll lift here. You have no hope of getting away. You're done for. There are two cars stuffed full of cops out there. In five minutes every cop in Toulouse will be here; it'll be like a convention. Not counting the TV and radio people ...

He didn't move, keeping his arm held out, his hand locked on the butt of his revolver.

I kept talking.

— Be sensible. So far you're up for attempted armed robbery. It's a serious charge but we can do something about it if you don't shoot. I'll be called as a witness at the trial. The evidence of a cop at the scene is worth years inside. If I tell them you put up no resistance, it'll get your sentence cut by three or four years . . . You've had it. Make the best of a bad job, it's better for everyone concerned.

My speech seemed to make no difference to him, or else I'd been barking up the wrong tree. I decided to speed things up.

— That's the deal. I'm giving you thirty seconds to let me know if you accept my offer. Hurry up, thirty seconds isn't a long time.

I didn't take my eyes off his gun. I knew I'd won when his hand relaxed and opened. The gun fell on the floor with the hollow sound of a toy.

The jeweller rushed to his attacker's feet and picked up the revolver. He waved it in the air with a nervous laugh.

— It's plastic! I'd never have thought . . . It's still pretty scarey, just as much as a real one.

The thief took advantage of this brief interlude to lift his hands to his mouth. He forced something down with several swallows before throwing himself on the ground, his body twisted with violent cramps. I knelt to take a closer look at him.

— He's poisoned himself. Quick, call an ambulance. He's going to croak!

The jeweller turned pale.

— No, Inspector, this bastard has just swallowed my diamonds and pearls. He's guzzled more than thirty million. He's nuts!

Lardenne came into the shop followed by a herd of

uniformed police, guns at the ready. I stopped him in his tracks.

— We have to get him to hospital right away. See to it.

— Is he wounded? We didn't hear any shooting!

— It's not that, this fucker has made a meal of the shop's capital. He's got the most expensive digestive tract in the world.

The ambulance took us to the military hospital near the Saint-Pierre bridge. The diamond guzzler went straight into the care of the enterologist. The doc saw us after examining him:

— There's nothing to be done for the moment. I have to tell you it's the first time I've treated a patient with indigestion from precious stones. Normally we find objects of lesser value. Nails, pieces of glass, fork tines. It's quite unbelievable what people manage to swallow. And I'm only dealing with what passes by mouth! Colleagues who work on the other orifices could tell you a thing or two ... Men as well as women! I've often thought we should collect all the foreign bodies removed over the last ten years just in Toulouse and put on a little exhibition of perversity ... Your diamonds would go down really well.

— Sorry, but we have to get them back, they're material evidence. Will it take long?

The professor pursed his lips so we could see he was thinking.

— They're small. They're heading for the stomach now. We'll follow their progress by radio or sound probe, to protect him from too many X-rays.

The jeweller broke in at this point.

— I hope my stones aren't going to be ruined by rays or gastric juices?

The professor gave him a scornful little pout and made no reply.

— Over the next few hours they'll pass through the

second part of the digestive system into the intestines. It is a delicate stage that is not without risks. We can't discount the possibility of an intestinal blockage that requires surgical intervention. It can be tricky, I won't pretend otherwise.

— And if it all goes along normally?

— That's what I'm hoping. In which case you will get the stones back in three days at the outside. I'd say tomorrow, if I was sure our patient would cooperate...

— Meaning?

— We still have one possibility: we could give him a strong laxative to stimulate fast bowel movement. Of course, we can't administer such a treatment without the patient's agreement. Amnesty International wouldn't forgive us...

The fearsome prospect of surgical intervention persuaded the crook to swallow substances designed to speed up his natural functions. I took the precaution of posting a guard in the room where the mobile toilet was and ordered him to check the prisoner's excretions.

The jeweller was grateful for my suggestion that he keep the policeman company and help him with his task.

The stones and the pearls were recovered the next day, thanks to a purgative whose secret formula the enterologist had refined so as to eliminate all risk of side effects.

*

There was a telegram from Paris when I got back to the office. Dalbois had a lead on Roger Thiraud's executioner. This was to let me know I'd get a detailed letter later in the day.

I tried to get down to a pile of pending files, without much enthusiasm. A run of break-ins, two or three

drunk and disorderlies, a summons ignored. I killed
time checking the service records of station staff in
relation to the promotion scheme. I saw that Bourrassol
could expect promotion to Scale 4 of his rank, unless
Commissaire Matabiau made no allowances for his
offspring's pranks and kept him on Scale 3 for two
more years.

I started at every ring of the phone, at every knock at
my door. The postman came regularly at five with the
evening delivery, but I'd have rather he broke with
routine. I rushed on to the stairs as soon as I saw him
come through the door. I took all the post and spread it
across my desk. Dalbois' letter was there all right. In my
haste I tore the envelope as I opened it. The Inspector
from Intelligence didn't bother with meaningless
formalities.

Dear Cadin,
Your CRS guy is called Pierre Cazes and it turns
out he was in the Special Brigades who had the job
of liquidating the OAS and FLN leaders during the
last years of the war. I should tell you that
everything connected with the Algerian war has
been covered by a decree of July '62 which
stipulates, among other things, that nobody can be
prosecuted or discriminated against in any way in
respect of actions arising from the events in
Algeria and Metropolitian France before the
proclamation of the ceasefire.

Pierre Cazes is retired now. Only a few
months ago he was living in your area, at Grisolles,
a village between Grenade and Verdun on route
17.

Watch your step, you're not walking on eggs any
more, but on a powder keg. Do me a favour,

destroy this as soon as you've read it, I've done the same with the photo you gave me.
Regards
Dalbois

I took a lighter out of my drawer and burned the letter and the envelope in the ashtray. I gave the rest of the post to the secretary for distribution. I set out to look for Lardenne.

I found him hunched on the front seat of the squad car. He seemed stricken by some nervous disease. His arms were shaking and his head jerked forwards. He would momentarily draw himself up only to lunge back down towards the wheel. This display of St Vitus Dance was explained once I got to the car. Sergeant Lardenne had abandoned the mathematical joys of the Rubik cube, to place himself in the nervy thrall of Bansai's video delights. In his hands he held an electronic board the size of a calculator and was trying to steer a small figure along a route strewn with ambushes.

— Let me see that, Lardenne! Head for Grisolles. It's a village on Route 17 before Montauban.

I left him to play with the white lines, the traffic lights, the highway code and all the little fellows who were driving around between Toulouse and Montauban this late afternoon.

I took over the escape of the little pacman, right thumb to go forward, left thumb to go back, and tried to get him as far as the helicopter that was waiting for him on top of the building. He had to climb a fearsome number of steps, pass through an infinity of doors that chose to shut as he got to them, forcing him into breathless detours. The concierge was there too, pursuing him with an avalanche of kitchen utensils. He also had to watch out for an enormous rat which relished nothing more than eating up whole floors!

On our way through the village of Verdun I managed to get my pacman on to the platform, but at the last moment the helicopter, unbalanced by a wrong movement of my right thumb, crashed against the windows of the 113th floor, while the gleeful concierge took advantage of this to stick a horrifying butcher's knife in the pacman's back. The rat rushed to gobble up the corpse. The gadget squeaked out the first few notes of the Funeral March.

— What was your total, Inspector?

I pressed the score display button.

— Nine hundred and thirty-nine steps!

— My personal record is one thousand five hundred and fifteen. It's a tough one . . . One of these days I'm going to treat myself to Yakoon. They say it's ten times more exciting. The little man has to face an enemy without knowing what he looks like, and who unleashes his different creatures on him. You never know if what's in front of you is a friend or an enemy. If you eliminate your helpers you're even less protected. You have to go through twelve different tests to get to the supreme combat with the Yakoon. What's more, the method of scoring varies with each game. It permutates to infinity. You need at least two months to master the first level. It's a fantastic game!

— Did you take a look at the signpost, Lardenne?

— What signpost, Inspector?

— The Grisolles road! You've just passed it. And you don't have twelve different options for getting back on it. There's only one: turn back the way we came!

·

Pierre Cazes lived in a little cottage surrounded by a pretty, well-kept garden. I went up to the gate and rang a little bell nailed to the gatepost. A man of around sixty with strongly marked features appeared at the ground floor window.

— Yes, what do you want?

— I'm Inspector Cadin from Toulouse. This is my assistant, Sergeant Lardenne. I want to have a word with you in private.

He came out onto the steps and used an electronic command mechanism to open the gate. I went up the path with Lardenne behind me. He met us at the door.

— To what do I owe the honour of a police visit? Not bad news I hope. My wife has gone out shopping in the village, but I can still offer you an aperitif.

We were in a vast room furnished in impeccable taste, with a stone chimneypiece as its focus. He placed several bottles on the table while he talked, then two glasses and a variety of savouries.

— There are only two glasses because I'm forbidden drink. I make up for it with my medicines.

He served us drinks, pastis for me, *floc de gascogne* for Lardenne, who likes sweet things.

— Well, Inspector, is it me you're investigating? Or my wife?

— No, not exactly. Would you mind us taking a little walk in the garden? I'd like to stretch my legs.

Pierre Cazes looked a little surprised but he agreed to my suggestion. I decided to get straight to the point.

— Right. In the first place, my being here has no official status. There's nothing I could do if you refused to answer my questions . . .

He made a sign to me to go on.

— During the last month a young man was killed in Toulouse . . . Bernard Thiraud . . .

I watched his face but his features displayed no particular emotion at the mention of the name.

— He was murdered in the street, with no apparent motive. We've checked everything, no connection with money or personal problems, nothing. A complete mystery. Then when I was questioning the family it came to my attention that the father of this young guy died in similar tragic circumstances twenty years ago. Murdered in the street: a bullet in his head. At the time there was no inquiry into this murder. By an enormous coincidence a Belgian television crew that was there for Jacques Brel's concert at Olympia filmed the last moments in the life of Roger Thiraud, Bernard's father. It happened in Paris in October 1961. Everything suggests it was you who held the gun . . .

Pierre Cazes thrust his hands in the pockets of his overall and clenched his fists. His shoulders sagged. He closed his eyes and, through parted lips, gave a deep sigh, then he stooped forward. With difficulty he sat down on one of the large stones that bordered the path.

— How did you find out? All the archives are top secret . . .

— By chance, I told you.

— Take a seat Inspector. You're stirring up very painful memories. I never expected a blow like this. What's the use of taking every precaution if it's fated; there's nothing you can do. What do you want me to tell you? Yes, I'm the one!

— Why did you kill Roger Thiraud?

For a split second his eyes became unfocused.

— I know damn all. I had orders. I had to obey them.

— Did they come from the Special Brigades?

— Why do you ask me if you know the answer? Yes, from the Special Brigades command . . . We had the job of cleaning out the most active leaders of the OAS and the FLN. The Préfecture supplied our passes and unmarked weapons. If there was any snag we had the Director of the Sûreté's direct number. I can still remember it, useless though it is now. MOGador 6833. We learned everything by heart, nothing in writing. It wasn't much fun, we lived a secret life. The other side didn't take anything lying down. An eye for an eye. It bears no resemblance to your job, Inspector. We were on our own, with our own methods of extracting information and operating.

— Even for the business in rue Notre-Dame de Bonne-Nouvelle?

— No, it happened regularly that we'd be picked out by central command to get rid of some underling who was in the way. I far preferred the other side of the job, liquidating the enemy. But taking out an ordinary guy never gave me any satisfaction. I can't speak for the others . . . You know I took part in the Resistance and the Liberation. I was active in Indo-China. I've been used to looking danger straight in the eyes: shooting a German or a Vietnamese in the belly isn't particularly pleasant, even if he was about to do the same to you. But sticking a bullet in the head of a young French guy you know nothing about. With him unarmed and from behind. It had to be done. I console myself with the thought that what I did maybe prevented a terrorist attack or shortened the war by an hour, a day . . .

— What exactly happened with Roger Thiraud? Who singled him out for you?

— The same as usual. A liaison officer left an envelope in a letterbox that I visited twice a week. That's where I found instructions and procedure. With Thiraud, if that was his name, I was supplied with a photo of the target and details of his movements, his routine. I chose to do the job during the demonstration. He lived near one of the rallying points; normally he ought to have been home before it started. I'd had it in mind to telephone him with some excuse to get him to come outside. But I didn't need to do that. He didn't go straight home, he went to a cinema opposite the Rex. I very nearly did the job during the film . . . Thinking about it now, I should have, I'd have avoided being filmed by a Belgian television crew.

— Didn't you want to know why this man was going to die by your hand?

— Why, do you think the OAS worried about that when they blew apart a dozen of my best buddies with thirty kilos of plastic planted in their meeting room? We picked them up in little pieces — I could hold the biggest in my hand . . . Or when they threw a grenade into a school playground? I've seen children's faces torn to shreds by bombs . . . Have you ever heard the screams of five-year-old kids blinded, solely to terrorise people? In those days I made a point of asking no questions so I wouldn't get ten times madder than I was.

— Who sent you these envelopes? You can tell me, it's twenty years now, part of history . . .

— I can't say for sure. Everyone knows that the Special Brigades were headed by André Veillut and that they were attached to the official police service, though they didn't appear on the family tree. The best proof is that my years of undercover work count towards my retirement pension. I can even tell you that they count double. But there were other groups too, like the SAC, which operated outside any hierarchy. Parallel commandos. We watched our step even though we were on the same side. Don't imagine time has erased the hatreds and resentments. I wouldn't be at all surprised if there were still old hands in the OAS trying to settle scores. The FLN not so much. They won, and the victors are always more generous than the conquered.

— So your boss, this Veillut, was probably behind the decision to wipe out Roger Thiraud?

— He would have to have known about it. Our chain of command reflected our commando-style organisation. It had to be as tight as possible so as to operate at top speed with the maximum chance of avoiding enemy intelligence. Veillut worked in a group of four, but he could act on his own in an emergency.

— What's he doing now?

— He'll soon be like me. He's close to retirement. When the Special Brigades were broken up, he got a post running the criminal investigation department in the Paris Préfecture. The government knows how to reward those who've served it well.

Suddenly, he bent towards the ground, beckoning me to do the same.

— Look, Inspector, an anthill. Two or three times a year I destroy it, to no avail; it's re-formed nearby. Have you ever looked inside one?

— Of course, when I was younger . . .

— It's strange, they build galleries and access ramps. I've read that there are more than two thousand species of insects classified as ants. Red ants, black ants, honey ants, driver ants, Amazon ants. When you look at them closely you can't miss noticing that there's some species or other which corresponds exactly to your own character. A little while ago I discovered what kind of ant I was . . .

He took a twig and pointed it at the edge of a small crater hollowed in the sand, as big as a five-franc coin and scarcely any deeper.

— The lion ant. A solitary! He digs his hole, gets into it and waits patiently in ambush for creatures like himself to fall within his reach . . .

The twig whipped furiously at the ground. An avalanche of sand covered up the lion ant. I stood up. Pierre Cazes gazed at me in mute mockery. I broke the silence.

— Thank you for agreeing to this conversation, Monsieur Cazes.

Sergeant Lardenne joined me, pastis on his breath. He was the worse for two aperitifs! He turned the car round in haste and got on to the Toulouse road.

I caught a glimpse inside the garage where a huge metallic green Mercedes sat in state, a 250SE from the sixties, with a chrome radiator. A dream car!

I turned to Lardenne.

— What a car! Some have all the luck . . .

— Don't believe it, Inspector. His wife arrived when you were talking in the garden. She thought we were from the hospital. The old guy hasn't got long to go; did you take a look at him? The docs give him three or four months . . . Another one who won't be enjoying his retirement.

— It's hard to believe. He's pretty cheerful for someone who knows he's a condemned man!

— He doesn't know how seriously ill he is, they've got him believing it's a bad ulcer.

Befor the bend I looked back. I could see an old woman dressed in grey standing at the garden gate. I had the impression she was making a note of our car number. Lardenne turned. She disappeared from sight.

.

The wall opposite the station had always carried echoes of events that shook the world. During frequent periods of reflection, my gaze would wander across the stones, where I read and re-read the white letters of FREE HENRI MARTIN, or traces of a half-obliterated slogan: . . . I AU REFERENDUM, without being able to decide whether the I was the last letter of OUI or the final stroke of an N for NON. As for this Henri Martin, I didn't know which of them to choose from all the different Martins in the dictionary:

Was it Henri Martin 1830–1883, born in Saint-Quentin,

French historian (*History of France, 1833–1836*) member of the Collège de France. Or Henri Martin 1872–1934, born in Dunkirk, French symbolist poet, *The Lily and The Butterfly* (1902), Académie Française Prize in 1927 for his collection *Vegetables and Shellfish.*

Or again, Henri Martin 1912–1967, born in Saint-Denis, French architect. Renovation of Paris. Project for the outer ring road.

I was still undecided the day Bourrassol, who had been getting acquainted with sea-faring lore ever since his son had gone to sea with the French fleet, informed me that the Martin whose name was on the wall had experienced the damp of a ship's hold and the hardship of chains for having refused to fire the several hundred shells under his control on the working-class districts of Haiphong, in the early fifties.

But the wall didn't only live in the past.

At the end of June a team of propagandists of Shi'ite persuasion had traced in white letters an imposing inscription: SOLIDARITY WITH IRAN.

Some other graphic artists, probably in disagreement with Khomeini's outlook, had simply crossed out 'Iran' and replaced it with 'Palestine'. The response of the Zionist students was to cover up 'Palestine' and take over the slogan by inserting the word 'Israel' outlined in blue letters.

Finally a genius came along and created unanimity by rollering over the words Iran, Palestine and Israel. For good measure this person also whitewashed 'WITH', leaving only the word 'SOLIDARITY'.

Commissaire Matabiau was back. He burst into my office on the dot of ten, without giving me the time to greet him with a friendly good morning . . .

— Come with me, Cadin. I want clarification of what's been going on here while I've been away.

He was in a foul mood. The Corsican suntan barely

covered up his bilious hue. He didn't hold the door for me as I followed him into his office; it just missed hitting me smack in the face. Matabiau sat leaning against the edge of the desk and crossed his arms on his chest. He must have got out of bed in a rush, for I noticed one of his socks was on inside out.

— Well Cadin, I'm waiting!

— There's been nothing really noteworthy, Commissaire, apart from the gravediggers' strike.

I was stalling for time, so as to find out whether Cazes had already made a complaint about my visit.

— All in all the strike only lasted a week and everything was quickly back to normal. A few brawls between the strikers and the mourning families. Otherwise run of the mill stuff. Complaints of all kinds, no need for me to draw you a picture. I've personally devoted most of my time to the biggest case of the month. The murder of Bernard Thiraud. There's a complete file on my contacts, in Paris as well as Toulouse . . .

— That's all?

He uttered the question in an exaggerated tone of voice, waving his arms about.

— Yes, I can't see anything else of significance. I won't go into the hold-up in allée Jean-Jaurès; there are pages of it in the newspapers . . .

I had dropped this in deliberately; the journalists were all going on about my courage in the face of an armed gangster; keeping quiet about the exact nature of the pistol I'd had pointed at me. Just the mention of my most recent exploit had the effect of softening the Commissaire's attitude.

— Yes, Cadin, I've read all those papers. I congratulate you on your presence of mind in the circumstances. What I'm really bothered by is this business of the situationists. I'd hardly got back from holiday when I was besieged by phone calls from the mayor, and his deputy, Prodis. Watch out for that parasite...I couldn't make sense of what they were on about except that Sergeant Bourrassol is supposed to be implicated in this business. I've never heard anything more out-landish! Can you imagine Bourrassol as a situationist? Do you know what this story's all about? Can you tell me what's behind it?

I put the staff-sergeant in the clear.

— Bourrassol had nothing to do with it. They're making things up just to piss you off. What's happened is that we're on to the network of situationists behind the fake municipal papers from 1977 onwards, as well as the bogus newspaper poster. Bourrassol's son was mixed up in that crowd, but he's got nothing to do with the fake summonses sent from the Commissariat. He has a cast iron-alibi: he's swanning about between Martinique and Guadeloupe courtesy of the cruises organised by the navy.

Commissaire Matabiau shot up off the desk and stood in front of me.

— False summonses! So this is what's up! Don't you think this is more important than anything else? I don't give a damn about your murder and your jewel eater. Before I went on holiday I had my suspicions you might land me in the shit. What exactly is going on with these falsified documents?

— We're still looking. Several hundred Toulouse residents received notification, a perfect forgery of an official form, telling them to make an urgent visit to the station in connection with the anti-terrorist records. The summons was signed in your name with what looked like your signature. It so happened that the recipients of this communication were chosen from among the most prominent personalities in the city. Big businessmen, industrialists, clergy, club men, notably the ex-servicemen's associations ...

— Can you show me one of these summonses?

I pulled my wallet out of the back pocket of my jeans and with some delicacy extracted a blue square which I unfolded before giving to Matabiau. He looked over it, line by line, in silence. This moment or two of study calmed him down, to my great astonishment. He handed the summons back to me.

— It isn't a fake. This form is quite authentic. I signed it the night before I left for Corsica. I don't know how this mess has happened!

I really think my surprise couldn't have been any greater if he had confessed to being Bernard Thiraud's murderer.

— I haven't lost my marbles yet, Cadin! I have a clear memory of giving the original of this letter to Sergeant Lardenne and also the list of the four hundred people concerned in Toulouse. I thought you had enough to do already with all the station paperwork without dumping this extra duty on you. All Lardenne had to do was make photocopies and make sure they got sent out ... Get him for me, I want to clear this up at once.

The sergeant was finishing off a pinball game in the café nearest the station. At the risk of making an enemy, I pulled him away from the machine's winking lights a hundred points short of a free game. I put him in the picture on the way back to Matabiau's office. The Commissaire had adopted a mournful expression. He raised his head when the door opened.

— Lardenne, you owe me an explanation. Try to make it a good one if you want to avoid a transfer to sentry duty! I suppose Inspector Cadin has brought you up to date? What do you have to say in your defence?

— I don't know ...

— Well, you'd better put your mind to it, Lardenne!

— I took the work to Madame Golan, one of the secretaries. I told her what you wanted. Word for word . . .

— Well done, Sergeant! I entrust you with a job of the greatest importance and you waste no time dumping it on the first person you can find! Go and get me this Madame Golan.

Lardenne was away for less than a minute. He reappeared accompanied by the large matronly lady who for many years had presided over the issue of ID cards and passports. She took up a not inconsiderable amount of space, but was none the less trying to be as unobtrusive as possible. This appeared to be the second time in her career that she had crossed the sacrosanct threshold of the boss's office, the first being when she was taken on. It was clear from her demeanour that she fully appreciated the gravity of the occasion. Matabiau displayed great sensitivity: without too much trouble he managed to shed light on the mystery. The poor woman was goodness itself. She had soon become known for acting well beyond the call of her ID card duties. She would seldom refuse to help out a harassed colleague; there never passed a day without someone asking her to give them a hand because of pressure of work, always adding 'I'll do the same for you' for the sake of form. Good Madame Golan folded papers, taped packages, indexed cards, and stapled things together for the whole police station.

When Lardenne turned up, flushed with the importance of his task, and asked her to send out four hundred summonses for the anti-terrorist records for Commissaire Matabiau, she accepted with alacrity, thanking the sergeant for having thought of her when it came to such sensitive work.

She did the same thing the next day when another section head asked her to help with the despatch of three hundred and seventy-eight announcements reading as follows:

The Benevolent Fund of the Toulouse police and the whole of the city's Police Force thank you for your generous gift which will be used, as in other years, to relieve the distress of the widows and orphans of our colleagues who have given their lives while safeguarding the public.

It wasn't known how the 'anti-terrorist' list came to replace the labels of names of the benefactors. But if the upper crust of Toulouse complained bitterly of being tainted with some shadowy international threat, no bomber, or suspected one, expressed his surprise at being thanked for a non-existent charitable donation.

Lardenne left the office first, closely followed by the secretary. Matabiau strode back and forth across the room raging against his subordinates and admin in general.

— Do you realise, Cadin, one hour back at work and I've already lost all the benefit of my holidays. It's put me on edge again, in one fell swoop. One month of peace, relaxation, it was too good to last . . . I'd have preferred it to have been Bourrassol's son who took the rap. At least he wasn't one of us. We look like fools. What'll they take me for? An incompetent? This Lardenne has got it coming to him. He'll find out about sentry duty. I can promise you! Right, there are other things to deal with, how's this murder going?

— Not as well or as fast as I'd like. We haven't much to go on. Bernard Thiraud was killed by a Parisian of around sixty. We have the statement of a witness who saw the murderer getting out of a black Renault 30TX registered in Paris, and following the victim. That took place opposite the Préfecture a few minutes before the

murder. Lardenne checked every likely location between Paris and Toulouse, motorways and highways,
but nobody remembers seeing the car or anyone
answering the murderer's description.

— If this was Lardenne's work, it's best to double
check . . .

— I'm not defending him, but I trust him with this
work.

— All right, go on.

— We haven't got very far with establishing the
motive. The young guy was on his way to Morocco with
his fiancée . . .

— I can't see why a Parisian would go through
Toulouse on the way to Morocco! It isn't the most direct
route to Marrakesh.

— No, indeed; Bernard Thiraud and his fiancée are
historians. They made a detour through Toulouse to
look up the archives in the town hall and the Préfecture.
Wads of paper on regional history. I worked there for
two days with Lardenne and came up with nothing.
However, I went to Paris and discovered a few things
that were more interesting. The victim's father was
killed in strange circumstances in October 1961, during
a demonstration organised by the Algerians. I can even
tell you that he was professionally executed.

— Who by?

— It appears to have been a political killing. Reasons
of State. I found the officer who was given the job. He
lives in an out-of-the-way place on the Montauban
road. He's retired. At the time he was in the Special
Brigades; there were undercover commandos created
by the ministry to take care of the OAS and FLN
leadership. When required, to take them out for good.
The service was headed by André Veillut, a high-up in
the Préfecture. Naturally, they fixed things so as to
avoid autopsies and investigations. The files are empty.

I don't know if it would do any good to fill them; all those things are covered by an amnesty decree.

— But you think these two affairs are linked, is that it? It's not too hard to construct a hypothesis whereby the son managed to identify his father's murderer and came here to avenge him. That would explain his itinerary.

— I'd be quite happy with that, but too many details don't fit. Firstly, Pierre Cazes. Apart from his age, he doesn't match up with the witness's description. I don't see him complicating the job unnecessarily by getting himself a car registered in Paris to come and commit his crime in broad daylight at maximum risk!

— If he's a professional, and we're dealing with a top class professional, this is exactly the kind of reasoning he would want to see you follow. The killer knows exactly what he is doing, Cadin. If you haven't found any trace of this Renault 30TX, maybe it's because it never made the Paris-Toulouse trip!

— It must exist though! No vehicle of this type was stolen during the weeks before Bernard Thiraud's death. I checked the national list myself.

— Why wouldn't someone have lent him the car? Do some digging on how Pierre Cazes spends his time and see whether one of his friends drives a black Renault... Did you go back to the archives after you turned up this Algerian demonstration story?

— No. Why, should I?

— In your shoes I'd treat myself to another session dusting off the files. Now you know what you're looking for: a link with this Pierre Cazes or the Special Brigades. That's worth the bother of two or three hours rummaging. You've a faint chance of unearthing an explanation. But you may come back empty-handed if the victim was really just there in his capacity as historian . . . In which case the Thiraud affair will remain a mystery. Until the day we come across a life insurance policy or a little letter breaking off a romance. The best crimes are often the most banal. Don't you think?

— Not this one. There are too many coincidences and ramifications. I know my real job is to find Bernard Thiraud's murderer, but the one thing I desperately want to get to the bottom of is why a mere teacher at the Lycée Lamartine ends up getting bumped off during an Algerian demonstration by a political cop disguised as a CRS man. If I had the guts I'd go and ask André Veillut what it all meant — the old boss of the Special Brigades! It's all been amnestied, he has nothing to lose by talking . . .

— I won't give you lessons in how to handle a case, Cadin, though I'll never give up handing out advice. Listen, please yourself how you work; you can go right back to the Siege of Alésia or the Saint Bartholomew Massacre if you think fit and it leads to the culprit's arrest! The point is to reach a solution: I don't give a damn which route you take to get there. But if you stray so much as a centimetre from legality don't count on me for cover. Say it loud and clear that it's Cadin's work and nobody else's. I don't want my name mixed up in any funny business! Take it as read.

— I've always taken responsibility for my work, Commissaire. I'm convinced these two crimes are connected.

— For now the only link is blood ties. Nothing allows you to extrapolate from that. Be very careful. You've just referred to TWO crimes, yet less than five minutes ago you were admitting that Roger Thiraud's death was covered by an amnesty. Watch your step very carefully, Cadin.

— I'll try, Commissaire.

— It's not enough to try. Above all, don't go on your

hunches. Leave that to the examining magistrates. I need an accused every bit as convincing as the corpse picked up beside Saint Jérôme's church. At any rate it would be better if you stayed in charge of the station while you get this case sewn up. You'll have more room for manoeuvre. I've still got two or three days' holiday. I was going to take them for some pigeon-shooting, but there's nothing to stop me using them this week! What do you think?

It was more than I could have hoped for.

— Fine by me. It won't be time wasted.

All the same, I had the funny feeling there was an ulterior motive behind this sudden generosity. Matabiau confirmed my suspicions.

— I'll make the most of it to do some home decorating. There's always something to be done when you've got a house. One last thing, Cadin, see Prodis about his business of the mixed-up letters. I'm counting on your sense of diplomacy to get it all sorted out.

CHAPTER EIGHT

I kept my part of bargain as a matter of urgency with a phone call to the deputy mayor. Prodis gave me less than ten seconds before fiercely interrupting.

— Inspector, I couldn't care less about your four hundred thank you cards! It's neither here nor there... We thought we had them after we found the plates at the municipal print shop. Well, we didn't. The offset machine minder must have given us a list of names selected at random. And their subversive activities are getting even more out of hand. We keep hearing about people getting letters from NIIEE announcing the annulment of the Toulouse census by a decision of the Ministry of the Interior. I'll read you the letter...

I heard what sounded like paper being unfolded.

'Due to a large number of confidential files having found their way into the possession of a group known as NIIEE (National Intervention Into Electronic Equipment), and a lack of vigilance in the town hall's recruitment of census personnel having allowed the infiltration of certain individuals who have taken advantage of computer loopholes, with the aim of causing damage to the system compiling individual records, and to social planning, the census is annulled throughout the Toulouse area.'

They then advise people to go to the town hall to reclaim their files! This isn't four hundred people we have on our hands, but at the very least ten thousand from our first estimates!

I got off the line fast and left Prodis to his paranoia. I rang Bourrassol. He had patiently explored the possibility of Bernard Thiraud's murder being a simple matter of mistaken identity with the victim being the wrong target. Having done a meticulous piece of work, Bourrassol was able to draw up an almost comprehensive list of people present in and around the Préfecture on the day of the murder between 4 pm and 6 pm.

— You know, Inspector, instead of planting our guys under cover in the hot spots, it would be better to get them jobs as receptionists in the entrance hall of the Préfecture. The list I've drawn up is unbelievable. A dozen big fish, people we never manage to collar, who are parading around undisturbed just outside the Prefect's office! Joe Cortanze, for instance, if I'm right there's a warrant out for his arrest for armed robbery?

— Yes, that's right.

— That doesn't stop him from being seen quite officially by the Deputy General Secretary and the Cabinet leader!

— Come on, Sergeant, you've been in this game long enough to know that our results depend 95 per cent of the time on what our informers tell us. You've just turned up lucky. You've got a few lookouts posted round the secondary schools to keep an eye on the dope traffic, haven't you?

— Yes, but not on this level!

— Otherwise?

— I've rediscovered an old acquaintance, ex-Sergeant Potrez. He has a vague resemblance to Bernard Thiraud. The same kind of heavy-set looks. He's about five years older, but for someone working from a photograph it could be confusing . . .

— I don't remember this name . . . Potrez.

— He was a crack shot, the star of the second territorial brigade, until the day he opened fire on a motorcyclist without warning. He was undercover to set up a gang of car thieves, the BMW gang. A kid on a bike on his way through that part of town took fright when he saw a guy in plain clothes wandering about with a Magnum in his hands. He took off fast. A real slaughter. The police surgeon took out five bullets. They were lodged in an area no bigger than my hand . . . Potrez was run out of the force; he's working now as an armed delivery man. I remember from the papers the young biker's friends were saying they'd get Potrez . . . That's often how it is in the heat of the moment; things settle down later . . .

— Yes, or the scores get settled. It took a few years, but Tramoni got hit for Pierre Overney's murder. Even if there's one chance in a thousand of it leading us to the murderer, we have to stick with it. We'll see in the end if it pays off!

.

I made up my mind to get home early that evening. I went to bed straight after the eight o'clock news. I had a choice of TV programmes between *It's A Knockout*, with Bécon les Bruyères at Knokke le Zoute, a magazine programme on the renaissance of Lyric Art in the Vosges, and a debate on the staggering of summer holidays. With my video in Poitiers, I had no other option. I fell back on Gutenberg and rummaged through the bookshelves looking for something new to read. I came across the unfinished monograph by Roger Thiraud that Claudine had given me. I tried it for size, had a look at the cover and decided to open it. It wasn't strictly a book, just a mock up. It seemed meant to be reproduced as it was. Adorning the fly-leaf was the coat of arms of the town of Drancy, with above it a handwritten dedication: To Max Jacob.

The title was laid out in letraset:

> DRANCY from its origins to our time
> by Roger Thiraud
> Member of staff, Lycée Lamartine.

I leafed through the book quickly. A large number of pages consisted of blank squares pencilled in with notes. Roger Thiraud had allowed for the precise placing of illustrations, photos, maps and diagrams. For each of them he gave the source and bibliographical reference. The opening chapter devoted several paragraphs to the history of the Earth in the Mesozoic period.

The Commissaire hadn't gone this far back. He'd stopped at the siege of Alésia! I skimmed the page, following the gist of the text. '. . . The sea covered the Paris region. Clay and chalk deposits were left on the site where, thousands of years later, Drancy would rise up.'

I jumped forward several millennia to chapter three. I learned that the name of the town came 'from a Roman coloniser, TERANTIACUM, transformed into DERANTIACUM, DERENTI, then DRANCY'.

I amused myself tracing shifts in my own family name, backwards. I arrived at a satisfying CARADI-NATIACUM.

In the year 800, the township had no school and a population of only two hundred.

I skipped eight centuries of sowing and harvests, to make acquaintance with the first local celebrity: 'Crette

de Paluel, a pioneer of agricultural mechanisation', was
the alluring title of this chapter. Roger Thiraud allowed
a whole page for the reproduction of a bust of this
eminent sage. He noted: 'Get photo from Print Room,
National Library'. I immersed myself in the brief
biography of Crette de Paluel, 'born at Drancy in 1741,
he invented the circular saw, the root-slicer, the
chaffcutter, and the ridge-plough for potatoes. A great
friend of Parmentier, he was his equal in promoting the
potato.'

In the quaint but serviceable lyricism of these
paragraphs, Roger Thiraud was trying to end an
injustice, taking pains to establish the reputation of his
great man.

The Revolution had left no deep marks in the
furrows of Drancy, but the fall and explosion, on 16
October 1870, of an airship pumped up at the gasometer
of la Villette took up a great deal of space.

The contemporary period made up the second part
of the work. It opened with a quotation from *Les
Misérables* :

*Paris's centre, its ring of close suburbs, this was the
earth's compass to these children. Never do they venture
beyond it. For them, everything stops just outside the
city's gates. Ivry, Gentilly, Aubervilliers, Drancy; that is
where the world ends.*

I closed my eyes for a moment; these words brought
back the few hours spent with Claudine on the remains
of the fortifications.

Roger Thiraud rapidly passed over national political
events insofar as they didn't impinge on his native
town. He dwelled at greater length on the varying
political affiliations of the municipal representatives
and the building of the first modern facilities. In the

final chapters he shed light on the innovations of the pre-war mayors and their town planning projects. This was the construction of a vast garden city made up of several thousand individual and collective dwellings. A kind of ideal metropolis, a twentieth-century phalanstery in which all inhabitants would have at their disposal a whole range of collective services: schools, stadia, a hospital, crèches, shops . . .

Work began on the garden city in 1932; the town doubled its population, to nearly 40,000.

In 1934 an even bolder programme was launched: Drancy would house the first French skyscrapers! Five towers each fourteen floors high, a series of buildings laid out on a grid, and an imposing four-storey horseshoe-shaped block, assembled several hundred dwellings reached by some thirty stairways. The whole thing was christened The Seagull, after a nearby locality.

Alas, the hopes for community life which moved the spirits of the avant-garde architects were strangely fated.

The limitations of the techniques then used in construction became apparent and numerous faults appeared even before the apartments were let. While there were takers for the detached houses, the first French skyscrapers failed to meet with the success their promoters expected. Whole floors stayed empty despite the low rents.

It had to be acknowledged, the rabbits weren't ready for their cages! The whole development was sold off to the Ministry of Defence which garrisoned a regiment of Mobile Guards there.

I got up briefly to have a beer and take a break. Then I immersed myself once more in the story of Drancy Garden City. Roger Thiraud had a passion for his subject; there was no shortage of details.

For 1940 he gave the exact number of German

soldiers taken prisoner at the front and interned in the Seagull development. This was a revelation; the French army had managed to take prisoners during the phoney war.

But the Germans were soon in residence at Drancy. In a change of role; from captives they became captors. From the summer of '40 they imprisoned the tatters of the French and British armies along with Yugoslav and Greek civilians arrested in Paris. On 20 August 1940 The Seagull development officially became a concentration camp for French Jews in transit for deportation to Germany and occupied Poland.

Roger Thiraud quoted the figure of 76,000 people rounded up over three years within a few kilometres of the Place de la Concorde, and then deported to Auschwitz. He put the number of those who escaped this at less than 2,000.

Every week 3,000 people passed through Drancy, which was guarded by four German soldiers, assisted in their task by several dozen French auxiliaries. Roger Thiraud underlined the figure four.

He recreated the life of the camp with the help of press cuttings and interviews with survivors. I had to force myself to read certain passages.

When we talked about Drancy in front of the children, we invented a name so as not be frighten them. A jolly sort of name: Pitchipoi. Drancy was Pitchipoi.

The next page had a pencil line across it and an explanatory note: Reproduce the facsimile of the letter from the Commandant of Drancy to Eichmann announcing the departure of the first transport of children under two years old. (Transport D901/14 of 14.8.1942.)

Some of these documents had been kept together as an appendix in a brown paper envelope. I took out a note from the Food Office, dated 15 April 1943.

*In reply to your note of the 9th instant, we are honoured
to communicate the following information:*

1. Children under nine months: *347*
*2. Children aged nine months to three
   years:*   *882*
3. Children aged three to six years: *1,245*
4. Children aged six to thirteen years: *4,134*
*5. Quantity of milk currently consumed
   (monthly):*   *3223.50 litres*

*Because of an extremely volatile complement, the
above figures only give an approximate notion and the
number of children can vary from day to day plus or
minus 50 units.*

Another pile of papers bore the label, 'Figures to be
Compiled', in Roger Thiraud's handwriting. Long
columns of figures spread out under headings whose
starkness multiplied the tragedy: departure date,
transport, order number, destination camp, gassed on
arrival, H group, F group, survivors in '45.

The total tally of deportees was 78,853, the survivors
2,190.

The last table set out, region by region, the geographical provenance of those interned at Drancy; it
included some categorisation by age groups.

The Paris region came first, followed by South-
Pyrenees, well ahead of the North or Central regions,
whose Jewish population seemed to have escaped the
stranglehold of the Gestapo. The Paris region came top
everywhere in this sinister hit parade, except for the
first age group, that of children less than three years
old. While the vast majority of regions had between 5
and 8 per cent, Paris reached 11 per cent and South-
Pyrenees was over 12 per cent.

I closed Roger Thiraud's unfinished book feeling
deeply upset. It took me a long time before I ventured to

turn out the light. Sleep wouldn't come. I got up to watch the last TV news. I fell asleep as morning came and the street was already filling with the first sounds of the day's work.

Commissaire Matabiau was first on the scene, strangely dressed in a voluminous black cape, and wearing a hood. I knew it was him even without seeing his face. He was walking slowly, down the length of a corridor whose beginning melted into infinity. His mask caught the bluish neon reflections. Matabiau moved forward, his head drooping on his left shoulder. To a large crowd of wretched poor he was handing out little squares of green card adorned with Prodis's photo. I found myself in his path, naked. He drew my attention to the indecent state I was in, giving me a paper. Under the deputy's photograph I recognised the official stamp of the police station, but the words blurred as soon as I tried to decipher them.

I then turned to look at the other participants in this disturbing ceremony and had no trouble recognising a good half of those around me.

The mourning families mingled with the ex-strikers of the cemetery service, while a unit of Mobile Guards tried to extract a large gold nugget from the yellowish entrails of a laughing hippopotamus. Suddenly there was a deafening sound; high-pitched screechings and explosions that curdled the blood of everyone there. Matabiau vaporised into the flashing reflections of the floor tiles.

The corridor had grown wider; the walls, putty-like, throbbed to the rhythm of a heartbeat. The horizon darkened as a massive black Renault bore straight down on us, its wheels running on shining rails that seemed to spring from its movement.

A ghastly face, distorted by the shape of the windscreen, grimaced behind the wheel. I suddenly made out the features of Pierre Cazes. I was rooted to the spot and I closed my eyes so as to avoid my death. In vain. I saw straight through the screen of my eyelids. The CRS man was now in some kind of mad frenzy; he leapt up and down screaming. His mouth, his eye sockets, his nose were filled with thousands of black ants with phosphorescent legs. He pulled them out in thousands and threw them against the car's windows. In its crazy wake the car dragged an interminable line of wagons. Old wooden goods wagons whose contents shifted about with the violent jolting of traction. The end of the transport was made up of roofless containers that flew into the air and fell heavily on to the rails, spraying the air with the smell of dust. With each of these jolts, thousands of skulls white as chalk rattled out of the containers and burst on to the bottom of the corridor.

Claudine Chenet appeared at the edge of a wood to my left. With her was the archivist with the club foot from the Toulouse Préfecture. They managed to halt the headlong progress of the huge convoy, opening the sealed doors one by one. Hundreds of bleeding Algerians got out of the wagons. They formed long wretched lines for as far as the eye could see. A transport worker uncoupled the car and released an old woman from the box that imprisoned her. I could make out the first smile of Madame Thiraud when the train got under way. The wheels began screeching in unison, creating an unbearable wailing sound. Two monstrous hands were placed either side of the Renault's bonnet; the thumbs blocked the car's head-lights. I felt myself being sucked away, down into my bed. With vertiginous speed the whole scene melted into a tiny red dot at infinity. Fleetingly, I glimpsed a silhouette whose outlines were reminiscent of Sergeant Lardenne bent over the screen of a car-shaped pocket video game. Piercing music covered up the din of the train, echoing its staccato motion. Thousands of children's voices took up the rhythm as the convoy moved away: 'Pitchipoi, Pitchipoi, Pitchipoi, Pitchipoi . . .'

I woke with a start, covered in cold sweat. For a while I lay distraught, trying to cheat fear and forget these visions of death. I tried to will up other images, the walk on the ramparts, the meal at Dalbois's. It was futile. Claudine's face vanished, imperceptibly replaced by Bernard Thiraud's. Dalbois took on the features of Pierre Cazes. I got round my terror by taking up Roger Thiraud's book again.

He ended the story of The Seagull development in less than a page. Liberated in August 1944, from September the camp housed several thousand French people accused of collaboration with the enemy. Roger Thiraud named the best known personalities, from Tino Rossi to Sacha Guitry, who stayed a short time at Drancy in these circumstances. In 1948 work was begun to restore the buildings to their original use. In the appendix the author gave the title of a film, *L'Enfer des anges*, filmed in the project in 1936 with Mouloudji as its star.

Bernard Thiraud's contribution amounted to no more than a sketch of how his father's work might be completed for the period 1948–1982.

Sunlight flooded the room. I went over to the window; heavy black clouds rose on the horizon, heralding a storm. I stretched out on top of the bedspread, with my hands behind my head, and stayed like that, thoroughly dispirited, until eight o'clock. I swallowed an instant coffee then made up my mind to go to the station.

When I got there I found Sergeant Lardenne balanced shakily on top of a piece of metal furniture. He was taking down the huge roadmap of France, 1971 edition, that covered nearly the entire wall of the entrance.

— What are you doing, Lardenne, you're going to come to grief!

He turned and mumbled a reply. I couldn't catch a single word.

— Speak up, I can't make out a thing you're saying...

He lifted a hand to his mouth and spat out half a dozen pins.

— The Departmental Supplies Branch has sent us this year's map. All the new roads are on it, even the outline of the motorways planned up to '85. I'm chucking out this antique.

I stopped momentarily to admire the sergeant's skills as a handyman. He unfolded the new map and put it up on the wall, pinning it at every twenty centimetres. Once the job was done he got down off the filing cabinet and came over beside me to stand back and survey his handiwork.

— No comparison, Inspector; it brightens up the office a bit, don't you think?

I couldn't take my eyes off the lines of motorways criss-crossing France. The designer was into colour; the main roads were picked out in yellow with a double border of bright orange lines.

— Take a good look at this map, Lardenne. Do you notice anything about the motorways?

He looked plainly nonplussed.

— No, there's a good lot of them . . . Do you think they've made a mistake?

— Look closely. You can't miss it! Start the investigation again from scratch! Right now.

— What investigation, Inspector?

— How many are there, Lardenne! I'm talking about the Bernard Thiraud murder case. Go and question the motorway police between Paris and Toulouse and the service stations, the restaurants. In both directions. You've got your work cut out.

— But Inspector, they'll give me the same answers they did a fortnight ago. And that's not counting the ones with blank memories or the ones who'll tell me to get lost!

I stood under the map. I traced one of the orange lines with a ruler.

— Who's talking about questioning the same people. We were barking up the wrong tree the last time. Maybe he took the A6 instead of the A10 . . .

— That's absurd, it's 300 kilometres longer!

— It's worth a try, Lardenne. I want a phoned report this evening for the Toulouse-Paris run. Miss nothing out; make it a clean sweep! Call me any time you need to, either here or on my home number. Get Bourrassol to sign your orders. And good luck.

Lardenne left. I headed for the Toulouse Préfecture. I gave Lécussan's name to the receptionist blocking the way to the stairs; she let me through. When he saw me the head archivist gave me a friendly wave. Then, limping badly, he came over to meet me. With each step he made the effort to lift his club foot even though he could just have slid his shoe along the floor, saving himself the exertion, and avoided the painful effect disabled people's movements make on their onlookers.

— Inspector, I'm glad to see you again. Our old relics have their charm, don't they?

I waited until he was right beside me before replying.

— Yes, I'd never have thought so! I'd like to take another look at the documents from the other day, the ones that poor boy went through.

— Are you making progress? If the question isn't indiscreet . . .

— Oh, just checking. By the way, I believe you keep a record of people's applications to look things up?

— Of course. It's procedure in all French record libraries. Why do you ask, Inspector?

I made up a plausible explanation on the spot.

— It's something that occurred to Commissaire Matabiau. We're trying to get hold of a retired policeman who knew Bernard Thiraud's family. I'd like to see if his name crops up on one of your forms.

Lécussan was very helpful.

— I can take care of that; it's straightforward for me. That'll let you get on with the other files.

— No, there's no need. Thank you anyway. Show me where these records are kept.

— Behind you in the deputy archivist's office. Each reader's form is numbered, then filed in chronological order.

— No alphabetical file?

— No, that wouldn't be of any help to us. Anyway, it's a mechanical job; these records never have any function, but we're obliged by law to keep them.

The deputy archivist, a young woman whose face was hidden behind large tortoiseshell spectacles, gave me the forms for the current year. I had no trouble finding the card Bernard Thiraud had filled in with his name, the reason for his research and the references of the files he wished to consult: everything listed under DE.

I leafed through the forms for a while without finding anything resembling Pierre Cazes's name.

I gave the file drawer back to the archivist. A sudden inspiration made me ask for the 1961 run. In great excitement I opened the file at October. The shock of it took my breath away when I came across a form for 13 October 1961 filled out in Roger Thiraud's name.

I closed my eyes. I re-read it, calmly, so as to be sure I wasn't making a mistake.

Toulouse Préfecture
Record Library Date: 13.10.1961
Name of applicant: Roger Thiraud Resident: Paris 2e Reason for search: Personal Documents consulted: Everything listed under DE

I returned the file to the young woman.

— Have you found what you were looking for, sir?

— Yes, I think so. Thank you.

The chief was waiting for me in the bay, a box of files under his arm.

— That's the DE listing. They're exactly the same papers from your last visit. Maybe you'll have more luck. And did you find any sign of this retired policeman?

— No, I think Commissaire Matabiau was on the wrong track.

I spread the contents of the box on the reading table and sorted out the different folders. I put aside DEforestation, DEmarcation, DEfence, and DElousing to concentrate my attention on the dozens of items referenced DEportation.

I felt disgust in the face of the horror underlying these memoranda swapped by bureaucrats with the aim of perfecting the human disposal machine. A series of letters revealed the different stages of deportation for the Jewish children of the South-Pyrenees region. In the first instance, a letter from the 'Secretary dealing with Jewish questions' at the Toulouse Préfecture, signed only with the initials AV, asked Jean Bousgay, Minister for the Interior, if the German orders were to be carried out. These made provision for Jewish children whose parents had already been deported to be sent to Drancy.

The Minister answered in the affirmative. The 'Secretary dealing with Jewish affairs' in Toulouse gave his instructions to the local police to carry out the Nazi plan.

Such perfect functioning on the part of the local administration would allow this region to beat Paris to first place in their ghastly championship, far ahead of the rest of the country!

There was no document mentioning the name Pierre Cazes; I didn't feel up to double-checking. I replaced all the folders in the box. I knocked on the door of Lécussan's office without getting an answer. When I went round the shelves I couldn't see him or hear the unmistakable sound of his awkward walk. In the end I went to his deputy.

— Isn't the head archivist still here?

— No, M. Lécussan went out ten minutes ago. Do you want to leave him a message?

— There's no need. Just give him my thanks for all his help.

*

The first drops of rain took me by surprise on the steps outside the Préfecture. Gusts of wind growing stronger by the minute raised the dry dust that had accumulated on the pavement and in the gutters. I hurried to get back to the station and avoid the worst of the storm.

It hadn't turned six yet but it was dark. Thick clouds blackened the sky. The ceiling lights had been turned on in the duty room and their livid glow tinged the room with a sinister atmosphere. Lardenne's telephone call caught me in Matabiau's office, looking for the Toulouse phone directory.

— Inspector, maybe you were right; I think we've got a lead ...

— Where are you calling from?

— From Saint-Rambert d'Albon, on the A6 motorway between Lyons and Valence. I've done over 550 kilometres since Toulouse! It's a pretty spot, you get a view of the Rhône. It's not far from Mont Pilat ...

— You can read me the tourist office brochures next time, Lardenne. What did you find out?

— I'll know for sure tomorrow ... I've just met a motor cycle team who permanently patrol the motorway between Lyons and Avignon. One of the guys was on duty the night of Bernard Thiraud's murder. He was working together with another cop, which is why I have to wait until tomorrow.

— Come out with it. It's even worse than when you had a handful of drawing pins in your mouth!

— In a word, François Leconte, the cop in question, was busy checking a lorry driver's papers near Loriol, just beyond Montélimar. At 11.57 precisely ...

— He's got a hell of a memory!

— No, he gave the guy a ticket; the time's given on the docket stub ... While he was doing that, his colleague stopped a black Renault 30TX that was doing more than a hundred and fifty an hour ...

— Registered in Paris?

— I'll find out. Anyway, the driver was acting like he was a real big shot. He showed an official service pass, at least as far as François Leconte remembers. He was in the middle of filling out the ticket ...

— Question his colleague, the sooner the better!

— Precisely, that's the problem. He's been on holiday since the beginning of the week. I'm trying to find out where he is. It seems he's off having a nice time in Brittany, in a caravan.

— Great! Our only witness is out in the wilds, with no telephone . . .

— Do you want me to take a run over there, Inspector?

— No, keep pumping the motorway cops and try to get their pal's address out of them. It really looks like we're getting somewhere. The crime happened at six. He did 500 kilometres by midnight, including getting out of Toulouse . . . We're making progress, I can feel it. As soon as you've finished at Saint-Albert de Ranbon . . .

— Saint-Rambert d'Albon!

— If you say so. Right, as soon as it's done, go on to Paris. Wait for me at my hotel, I'll join you right away.

— Take the A10, Inspector, it's more direct! I still can't understand, if this really is our man, why he did the Paris-Toulouse return journey on the motorway to the south instead of going the direct route via Bordeaux. I've worked it out, Paris-Bordeaux-Toulouse there and back, adds up to 1,600 kilometres, while Paris-Lyons-Montpellier-Toulouse there and back is more than 2,200 kilometres. He surely didn't do an extra 600 kilometres just for the nice scenery?

— Mont Pilat doesn't come into this business, Lardenne, I'm sure of that at least!

— Why then?

— Because he's been the one making up the rules until now . . .

·

I had various matters to deal with urgently; I made up my mind to leave the station when the night squad came on. An oppressive heat had replaced the coolness brought by the late afternoon storm. When it hit the overheated tarmacadam the water evaporated and a thick clammy mist hung over the ground. I decided to

walk home. I went round Saint-Sernin church to head
down to the Garonne along rue Lautmann. The rush-
hour traffic of cars and pedestrians over the Saint-
Pierre Bridge had abated. I made for the Catalans
quarter, along the river, cutting out the detour through
allée de Brienne.

It was when I got as far as avenue Séjourné that I first
became aware of a presence like a delayed echo of my
own movements. I walked on another twenty metres or
so to make sure I wasn't imagining the shadow, then
turned round quickly to scan the embankment. A
figure was silhouetted in the light of a street lamp; the
contrasting brightness behind him made it impossible
for me to distinguish the features of the man who'd
been following me. He was short and seemed to be
leaning on his right leg. He was pointing a pistol at me, a
few particles of light were caught against the darkness
of the barrel. I realised there was another street lamp
less than two metres behind me. I could only be made
out in the same semi-darkness as my adversary. I eased
my right arm on to my stomach, and, judging every
little movement, unbuttoned my jacket. This provoked
no response from the man who had me in his sights. It
was patently obvious that he was using a gun for the
first time in his life; his limbs were stiff, his spine rigid,
he held the gun straight out level with my face.

At that distance the odds of hitting me were less than
one in ten. He should have been bent at the knees,
hunched forward with his right arm held in and aiming
at my chest, while steadying himself with his free hand.

I called out to distract his attention.

— What do you want? If it's money I'm willing to
throw you my wallet . . .

— I'm not interested, Inspector Cadin, I have no need
of money. You shouldn't have stuck your nose in . . . I
didn't want . . .

The voice was familiar, but I couldn't quite identify it. The man refreshed my memory with a forward movement of his club foot.

— You're mad, Lécussan. You won't get out of this alive. Drop your gun while there's still time.

The head archivist kept moving towards me with his jerky gait, pointing the pistol.

I'd had enough time to unfasten the holster. I dropped on to my left side gripping the butt of the Heckler as I went down. Instinctively, my forefinger slid on to the breech and released the safety catch before coming to rest on the trigger.

I emptied the first bullet from the magazine stretched out on the damp cobblestones of the embankment, while gunfire sprayed out of Lécussan's fist. The bullet whistled over my head. I pulled the trigger again and again, taking deep breaths, and not stopping to think about it. Only the fear of death made me fire. Lécussan had collapsed after his first shot. His gun had slid into a puddle. I got to my feet and went to pick it up. Turning it towards the light to lose the reflections, I made out the inscription on the barrel: Llama. Gabilondo. Y. Vitoria.

A model identical to the one used by Bernard Thiraud's murderer.

Lécussan was no longer alive. Two of my bullets, had shattered his skull, a third had got lodged in the club foot, just above the heel. I telephoned the station from a cabin on the embankment. I gave the duty officer strict orders to embargo the information for twenty-four hours.

Passers-by, intrigued by the sound of fire, had begun to gather, but none had the courage to approach me ... I wonder even if courage would have been enough!

As I walked away, I heard the sound of ambulance sirens mingled with those of the emergency services police van arriving at the scene of the shooting.

At half past midnight the Paris express left Toulouse
central station. I'd managed to get a couchette. I fell
asleep before Montauban, rocked by the complacent
snores of two commercial travellers.

CHAPTER NINE

They had gone to bed early as usual. She slept noiselessly; he watched her tenderly in the semi-darkness. All he did was toss and turn, irritated by the sheets and the heat of the mattress, unusually alert to the slightest murmur in the garden or the least creak on the stairs. It wasn't his illness that kept him awake, nor was it his doctor's last examination that afternoon.

He'd known for a while that he was being fooled. For exactly a year, when he'd come across the medical books his wife kept hidden in the attic. Then he noticed how she fell upon every little article.

He'd understood that his 'ulcer' had nothing to do with it, that it was the foul beast devouring him from inside.

He didn't let on, as if he was taken in by their little story. He was looked after, made a fuss of, spared the slightest effort.

In this way they had scrounged a year of happiness, a few dozen weeks reprieve . . . Eternity in other words!

No, his sleeplessness was caused by something else, by the visit of the little cop from Toulouse and all the memories, the disgust and shame it had stirred up in him. There wasn't a single minute he didn't think about it. Tragic memories passed through his mind, blocking out the happier ones he was apt to dwell on. He got up.

The disturbance woke his wife, who was immediately wide awake.

— Aren't you feeling well? Would you like some camomile tea?

Allaying her fears, he went straight to the telephone in the entrance hall. He dialled the station number Inspector Cadin had given him. The duty officer answered.

— I'd like to speak to Inspector Cadin, it's very important.

— The Inspector isn't in Toulouse, he went to Paris at short notice on a case.

— I don't believe it! The ba ... How can I reach him? Which hotel ...

— I'm afraid I can't help.

He put the phone down, thought for a moment, then quickly got dressed. He got down a cardboard box from the top of the wardrobe and from the oiled rag inside it took a Browning pistol, a 1935 model, his preferred weapon. He released the magazine to load its thirteen cartridges and snapped it back in with the flat of his hand.

His wife stood in front of him in silence. There was nothing she could say.

When he'd finished checking the gun he slipped it into his jacket pocket and went to the garage.

The metallic green Mercedes started first time.

Less than ten minutes later Pierre Cazes was on the motorway to Paris. Headlights raised, speedometer fixed at 180.

CHAPTER TEN

Sergeant Lardenne was finishing his breakfast in the hotel bar, and trying to solve the crossword in the *Figaro*. I watched him put his bread and butter down and fill in several clues one after another.

— Good morning, Lardenne, so you're a crossword addict too! You should go to the casino sometimes! You must have a yen for it . . .

He gave a start when he heard my voice.

— Inspector! In Paris already! I wasn't expecting you until this afternoon. You travelled overnight . . . Did you get any sleep?

— Yes, I got a couchette. Well, what about this motorway cop, did you get hold of him?

— Yes, last night round eleven. At the Marrek Rose camp site in Trebeurden. A gendarme from Lannion went there; he took him to the station in Trebeurden. I got him on the phone. The Renault 30TX was indeed registered in Paris; I have to contact vehicle records to get the owner's name . . .

— Didn't he take down details?

— No. As soon as he was stopped the guy flashed a service card and started sounding off about being on an assignment. The cop let him go on but he made a note of the number, force of habit. 3627 DHA 75.

— Good work, Lardenne. I'll take care of checking

out the name of the car's owner. You must rush to
Madame Thiraud, in rue Notre-Dame de Bonne-
Nouvelle. Ask her if she remembers a trip her husband
made to Toulouse in October 1961. A few days before
his death. Then go and collect Claudine Chenet from
her place. The two of you are to sit tight and wait for me
at the Café du Palais. It's by the Seine, just beyond the
Préfecture. I'll be there around two.

The morning was just long enough for me to go to the
vehicle records office, get the name the Renault was
registered in, find the vehicle and have a few words
with its usual driver.

I then got in touch with the man in charge of General
Services at the Toulouse Préfecture; he gave me the
answers I wanted. To wind up I paid a visit to Dalbois.

— Hello, Cadin. Did my letter get you anywhere? You
know it wasn't easy to track down your man; they keep
things quiet! Was it him?

— Yes, he executed Roger Thiraud in '61, under
orders. Though I don't think he's involved in the son's
murder. The fact is, the man I met is a sick pensioner
whose only concern was to be forgotten. Unless he's a
better actor than I gave him credit for . . .

— That's quite possible; your peaceful pensioner got
moving after your visit. I've heard about it from the
colleague who gave me his file. Don't trust his kind for a
minute. To have done a job like that he was no
choirboy! You'd better watch yourself . . .

— Maybe so. I'm keeping an eye on him, and I found
out a few things from our meeting. I think I've got my
man. One tiny piece more and the whole puzzle fits!

— And you think you'll find it here . . . Am I wrong?

— No, you're right. Look, it's confirmation I'm looking
for. I've made my mind up, but as you well know,
it's solid evidence that's needed. . . . Every member of
the force is followed by the administration, from the
day of entry into service to the day of retirement. I have

my file just as you have yours. Every year it surfaces for
our superiors' comments, right?

— Yes, naturally. I can't see how you'd manage a
force of nearly 100,000 men otherwise!

— I'm not criticising the system. Our entire career is
summarised in this document which is sent to the
Commissaire whenever people are moved. When I
came to Toulouse, Matabiau had immediate information about my previous conduct and how it was judged
by my respective bosses. Well, I'd like a photocopy of
one of these files. Is that possible?

— Your personal file? No, I can't do it; it's filed in
Toulouse! Here I only have access to the Paris records.

— I couldn't care less about my file; I know it better
than anyone does! The file I want to get hold of is on
someone working in the Paris Préfecture.

— That's better. I'll dig out one of the union representatives to take a quick look at the personnel records . . .

— You've got friends in the unions! I'd never have
expected it!

— Just a few. When you work in Intelligence you
have to know a lot of different people . . . Some are
unlikely but useful. The police unions are a world apart,
especially the smaller ones. When they get less than 10
per cent at the elections they have to find support. This
is where I come in. If they get bigger they can always be
reminded of contacts that may be embarrassing!
Everything's negotiable, especially honesty. Give me
your guy's name and wait for me in the corridor. I'll
bring you what you're after within the hour.

.

For lunch I made do with a souvlaki I bought at a
pseudo-Greek stand. I ate it as I walked to the Ile de la
Cité. Too many onions.

Sergeant Lardenne and Claudine Chenet were chatting as they sat relaxing at a table outside the Café du Palais. The young woman had changed into a dress and for the first time I saw her smooth, tanned legs. She got up as I approached.

— Inspector Cadin, what's going on? Your colleague won't tell me a thing. Are there any developments?

— Yes, we're close to a solution. I very much want you to be there when Bernard's murderer confesses. Do you feel up to it?

— Yes, let's go ahead.

I went into the Préfecture courtyard followed by Claudine and the sergeant. A metallic green Mercedes was parked in one of the VIP spaces. With a wave towards the archway, a uniformed doorman directed us to door C. A desk and chair had been stationed at the entrance and the man on duty stopped us at the bottom of the massive staircase.

— Can I help you?

I went over to him.

— We'd like to see Monsieur Veillut.

— The Director is busy. He's in a meeting. Do you have an appointment?

I said no. He held out a register and a ballpoint pen.

— Put down your name and the reason for your application.

I pushed the register back.

— We can't wait! I've come from Toulouse specially to meet him. Lift your phone and tell Monsieur Veillut that Inspector Cadin is downstairs and wants to see him right away.

He complied grudgingly and dialled the number for the Director of Criminal Affairs. When he put the phone down he lowered his head and spoke in an undertone.

— It's impossible, Monsieur Cadin. Try coming back later today or tomorrow . . .

I decided to by-pass him. The doorman tried to butt in front of me but I pushed him back roughly. The staircase was thickly carpeted; we went up without making any noise.

The dry crack of gunfire took us by surprise just as we reached the second floor, where Veillut's office was. Lardenne got his gun out at once, while my first reflex was to push Claudine to the ground. Then I took out my gun. A second shot rang out behind the door of the office. Uniformed cops burst on to the landing. At first they thought they were dealing with a group of killers; they aimed their guns at us.

I put my hands up.

— We're in the force too. I'm Inspector Cadin from Toulouse. The shooting's in the Director's office!

I pointed towards it with a wave of my gun.

Two policemen took up positions either side of the door. They were about to break it down but that wasn't necessary. It opened, making way for an old man whose face was distraught, as if he was suffering from some terrible, hidden injury.

Lardenne touched my shoulder.

— Hey, it's the retired guy from Montauban!

The cops hadn't moved, shocked by the sight of this tragic figure.

I went into Veillut's vast office. The Director of Criminal Affairs was no longer alive, a thread of blood oozing from his temple, dripping straight on to the thick blue carpet. A Browning was lying next to him, a pre-war, collectors' model.

When I went back into the corridor Pierre Cazes gave me a painful, tight-lipped smile.

— He would have got you first, kid ... The deck was stacked.

And they took him away.

·

A little later, when were were eating in a small Turkish restaurant near Sentier, Lardenne and Claudine crowded me with questions.

— They'll never know if he really was the murderer. How did you guess?

— There's no doubt though . . . It was Veillut who killed Bernard Thiraud on 28 July in Toulouse. He also ordered the murder of Bernard's father in October '61 when he was at the head of the Special Brigades.

— Are you certain?

— Yes. On 28 July, Lécussan, the head archivist in the Toulouse Préfecture, telephoned Veillut to let him know that a young man called Bernard Thiraud had asked to see the documents classified under DE. Just as twenty-two years earlier another Thiraud . . .

Claudine interrupted me.

— Do you call that proof? How can you be sure Lécussan telephoned him — he's dead too.

— Just a minute. There's no doubt about the phone call. The Toulouse Préfecture has an electronic switchboard; it has a system of sorting all calls and grouping them by department. It was installed with the aim of cutting costs by keeping a check on each employee's outgoing calls. Local calls are just totalled up, but long-distance and international connections are accounted for separately. On demand the system can supply a list of the calls made from any particular extension. Lécussan used extension 214. The tape recorded a call to the Paris Préfecture on 29 July at 8.46 am. If you want to be sure, call Trombel in General Services at the Toulouse Préfecture; he'll be happy to confirm it for you.

Claudine and Lardenne shook their heads nicely in unison. I was unstoppable.

— I think he asked Lécussan to get rid of Bernard Thiraud, but Lécussan used his disability as an excuse to refuse. Veillut was stuck. He didn't think twice. He left his office right away; his rank allows him this kind of privilege. We'd only need to question his secretary or the doorman for confirmation. Despite everything, I acknowledge he was pretty smart. Any run of the mill criminal would have rushed to Toulouse by the shortest route and we'd have been on to him long ago. The A10 motorway, Paris-Bordeaux-Toulouse! He played a canny game, suspecting the first thing we'd do would be to check all points on route. It was a good bluff choosing the long way round, the Sunshine motorway. A real scenic route: Paris-Lyons-Avignon-Carcassonne-Toulouse! Eleven hundred kilometres... Lardenne, you took the Bordeaux route in both directions to question restaurant and service station managers, cops and toll keepers. All for nothing. We thought we were on the trail of a ghost car. Who would have thought of a guy being so smart as to drive an extra 600 kilometres to blur his tracks? It nearly worked! It was the Departmental Supplies Section of Haute-Garonne that put us right, by accident! They had the nice idea of replacing our old wall map with one where the motorways are almost phosphorescent.

Lardenne's face lit up.

— I knew there was a connection.

I went on with my evidence.

— Veillut covered the 1,100 kilometres with his foot down. He only stopped to fill up the tank. He got to Toulouse before six, and parked in front of the Préfecture to wait for Bernard Thiraud coming out. Lécussan had given him a detailed description on the phone and fixed things to keep Bernard Thiraud there until the evening. When the young guy came out he followed him and killed him when the opportunity arose. He returned to Paris right away so that he could be seen in his office early the next morning. Unluckily for him, the best scenarios can't beat fate. This time it came along in the shape of a motorway cop near Montélimar . . . at . . .

The sergeant finished the sentence.

— Saint-Rambert-d'Albon.

— Thanks, Lardenne. At 11.57 precisely, that evening. It was the motorway cop who gave us the registration number of the car, a Renault 30TX. I've had a long chat with Veillut's chauffeur at the Préfecture garage . . . Like all professional chauffeurs, he keeps an eye on the working order of the tool of his trade. Especially since it's his baby if something goes wrong. He couldn't help noticing how the clock had jumped overnight between the 28th and 29th of July. More than 2,000 kilometres, it's plain enough! Especially since he'd planned to change the oil on the 31st: the car was coming up to 35,000 kilometres. Veillut never ever spoke to him, otherwise the chauffeur would have pointed out that the car pool chief had bawled him out because of the excess on the clock.

Claudine had been silent until now.

— It's funny, but his death doesn't even make me feel any better . . . I thought I'd be happy when Bernard's murderer was arrested . . .

I paid the bill for the three of us. Outside, I spoke quickly before she went off.

— We could have dinner together this evening, I'm not leaving until tomorrow morning.

She nodded towards Lardenne, lowering her voice.

— With the sergeant?

— No, he prefers electronic company. He can't wait until they develop a video plate!

— Okay. Let's make it eight o'clock. Pick me up at home. Do you remember the address?

— As if a cop of my calibre could forget such a vital piece of information!

CHAPTER ELEVEN

The magistrate charged Pierre Cazes that evening, a little after seven. It was thought he wouldn't live until the trial. A chance to bury the whole business. I went off to meet Claudine Chenet. She came to open the door. She didn't give me time to take in the room I was entering. She pressed against me and placed her hands on the back of my neck. My palms slid down her back. I kissed her with my eyes shut while my right foot pushed back the door on to the corridor. She pulled away from me without a word and sat down on the edge of the bed. I watched her, unsure of what to do. Tears were flowing down her cheeks.

— Why are you crying? It's all over, you have to forget . . .

— No, it's not why you think. I'm ashamed to be happy after all this. You can't know how much I've felt alone and abandoned since that day . . . I needed to have someone beside me . . . You most of all. It's a hard thing to say, but I can't get used to unhappiness, the way Bernard's mother has.

She smiled and kissed me again.

— There, that's it, I've stopped crying. Look, I've bought some fruit. Strawberries and peaches, do you like them?

I sat on the bedspread and took her in my arms.

— I've wanted the same, since we first met.

— I promise you I won't talk about it any more, but tell me why this old guy had it in for Bernard. And his father. I need to know. Is there something secret?

— No. The journalists must be sweating over it in all the Paris newsrooms! André Veillut had nothing against the Thiraud family. He saw Bernard only once, in Toulouse. I don't think he even knew Roger Thiraud ...

— Then he was a madman ...

No, just a bureaucrat. He began his administrative career in 1938 in Toulouse. He'd just turned twenty. He set his sights for the top, armed to the teeth with diplomas. In under a year he was made Deputy General Secretary in the social section: assistance to needy families. In 1940 he was in charge of assistance to displaced persons and the reception of those French people fleeing the German advance. In 1941 his brief was extended to Refugee and Jewish Affairs.

As a zealous bureaucrat, Veillut followed the Vichy government's instructions. He scrupulously administered the transportation of Jewish families to the transit centre at Drancy. Not out of political conviction nor anti-Semitism, but just by obeying the rules and carrying out the orders of the hierarchy. These days, dozens of obscure Section Heads decide what quantities of tomatoes or peaches will be dumped because of overproduction. As far as they're concerned the thousands of tons of fruit that are destroyed are nothing more than a figure and a code on a printout. In 1942–1943, Veillut was doing the same thing, feeding the Nazi death machine and liquidating hundreds of human beings, instead of regulating the agricultural surplus. Lécussan was working with him as a clerical administrator. A formidable team. The region they covered tops every other region in France for deportations of Jewish children. In other Préfectures, people tried to scramble the cards, to lay false trails for the Gestapo. Not in Toulouse. Veillut was anticipating their wishes. It was efficiency he was after. There'd never have been such a massacre if the Nazis hadn't benefited from the complicity of so many French people. They even got their hands on kids under two, despite them being spared by Pétain's decrees ...

— But Bernard's father was a child then, he couldn't have been involved in any of that.

— Roger Thiraud was born in Drancy, there's the connection. It's all it took! In his free time he was writing a short monograph on his home town, you know the little book you gave me. Apart from Crette de Paluel, Drancy was of no interest. Until the concentration camp that made it sadly famous. Bernard's father devoted a long chapter to it, as well as the initial architectural project of building a futurist new town. He checked hundreds of documents: architecture, statistics, lists of names. And then one day he noticed the disproportionate number of children deported from the Toulouse region. As a historian, he became determined to understand the reason for this imbalance. Maybe there had been a very big Jewish community, or a centre where Jews from different regions were assembled ... Roger Thiraud went to Toulouse, first to the municipal archives in the Capitole, then to those in the Préfecture. After a detailed study of the documents classified under DE, he soon realised that the responsibility for the inflated numbers of children fell on a high-placed Toulouse bureaucrat in charge of Jewish Affairs, identified only by the initials AV. He left for Paris again apparently intent on discovering the identity of this unknown person. Unluckily for him, the head archivist, Lécussan, was aware of his visit and the reason for his research. He immediately alerted Veillut that a historian was getting too closely interested in explosive documents.

Claudine interrupted me.

— But wasn't there an investigation to establish who'd been responsible for what, after the Liberation?

— Yes, of course. Veillut and Lécussan aren't fools. They proved it by staying above suspicion for more than forty years. At the start of '44 they sensed that the heyday of collaboration was nearing its end, that they'd soon have to account for themselves. They distanced themselves from Vichy and put their efforts into helping the Resistance networks. In the most showy way. When the Liberation came Veillut was decorated for valour! Nobody would venture to cast doubt on a man with a hero's rosette on his lapel. Since then, Veillut has never stopped climbing the ladder: General Secretary of the Bordeaux Préfecture in 1947, Head of the Prefect's office in Paris in 1958. In the course of 1960 he was entrusted with a secret mission: to set up a team with the job of liquidating the most troublesome FLN leaders. Its activities were extended to the OAS in 1961.

I took an apricot from the fruit bowl and went on.

— When in 1961 Lécussan warned him about the research being undertaken by Roger Thiraud, Bernard's father, Veillut quite naturally drew on the skills of one of his men, Pierre Cazes. Of course he neglected to reveal the real reason for Roger Thiraud's execution. Just a week ago this cop was still convinced he'd terminated a dangerous terrorist. Like a good professional, Pierre Cazes took advantage of the disturbances on 17 October 1961, the Algerian demonstration, to carry out his contract. Wanting to finish his father's book, Bernard reached the same conclusions about the children's deportation. He wanted to check the sources. With the result that he met the same end. But this time by Veillut's own hand. Twenty years after his father . . .

— Do you think this whole story will be published in the newspapers?

I couldn't answer that; I'd already been told to soft pedal it. At the Ministry they were drawing up a version more in keeping with the idea that the citizenry had of the guardians of public order.

— Maybe not everything, but they'll have to release a good piece of it.

Claudine leaned down and snuggled up to my chest. I stopped talking. I caressed her hair, gently, rocking her backwards and forwards, cradling her, to make her feel safe. I fell asleep a lot later, wrapped in the scent of her skin.

EPILOGUE

Lardenne went back to Toulouse without me. I'd treated myself to a day off. Claudine and I had gone out to get my suitcase from the hotel. Bonne-Nouvelle station was nearby. It was being renovated. A dozen workmen on scaffolding were busy tearing off the layers of posters covering the advertising hoardings. Further down, at the end of the platform, two other workmen were scraping the white ceramic tiles with metal spatulas. As it was torn away, the paper exposed ten, twenty-year-old ads.

A punk couple with brightly coloured Mohican haircuts were kissing under a poster that pictured the town of Savignac and boasted the benefits of Calvé oil: rich, light, and a hundred per cent vegetable . . .

A young executive, with an attaché case in his hand and a Walkman on his head, was strolling past a poster that spelled out a mineral water jingle: Badadi badadoi . . .

Claudine stopped in front of another bit of the wall. She pointed to a tile still partly covered in shreds of yellowing paper that an Algerian workman was having trouble getting rid of. Only some of the text was legible but its meaning was not lost:

. . . prohibited in France . . . liable to be sentenc . . . court

*mart . . . Ger . . . Anyone carryi . . . Jews . . . maximum
sentence of de . . . irresponsible eleme . . . support for the
enemies of Germany.*

*. . . ilance . . . guilty and the population of the occupied
territories.*

Signed: the Militaerbefehlshaber Stülpnagel.

Aubervilliers
January–February 1983